THE INTI
AN EDW

Also in this series

THE INTIMATE MEMOIRS OF AN EDWARDIAN DANDY
Volumes I–IV, VI

The Intimate Memoirs of an Edwardian Dandy

Volume V
Back to Basics

Rupert Mountjoy

Edited and Introduced by
ARTHUR GARVICE

WARNER BOOKS

A *Warner* Book

First published in Great Britain in 1995
by Warner Books
Reprinted 1998

Copyright © Potiphar Productions 1995

The moral right of the author has been asserted

*All characters in this publication are
fictitious and any resemblance to real
persons, living or dead, is purely coincidental.*

A CIP catalogue for this book
is available from the British Library

ISBN 0 7515 0116 6

Photoset in North Wales by
Derek Doyle & Associates, Mold, Clwyd
Printed and bound in Great Britain by
Clays Ltd, St Ives plc

Warner Books
A Division of
Little, Brown and Company (UK)
Brettenham House
Lancaster Place
London WC2E 7EN

This is for Abigail and Doctor Jonathan

Introduction

'IT IS TRULY REVOLTING, AS was done in a recent notable instance, that a man should be able to conceive of a woman describing her love for her husband to his young sister in these words: "My love for Henry is a purely sensual one",' thundered the Victorian literary critic Bernard Crackenthorpe in a review of *The Visitors At Twilight*, a long-forgotten three-volume novel by John Grahame. This angry attack was written around the turn of the century, when the spirit of Society was neatly summed up by Hilaire Belloc, writing: 'The husbands and the wives of this select society/Lead independent lives of infinite variety.'

Even during the late Victorian era, there was much toing and froing between bedrooms at the great country house weekend parties, and with the ascent to the throne of the fun-loving Edward VII, many members of the upper classes paid only the merest lip service to the repressive and often unpleasantly hypocritical morality propounded by the Establishment for the general population. For example, at the King's delayed coronation in 1902 (after his recovery from an

1

operation for appendicitis) a pew known as 'the King's loose-box' was set aside to accommodate several of his mistresses, including Lillie Langtry, Mrs Keppel, Lady Warwick and the famous French actress, Sarah Bernhardt. And, as the journalist Edward Pearce noted drily in *The Guardian*, in an article about recent sex scandals involving Government politicians: 'Sex used to be less controversial. Lord Hartington, the late Victorian statesman and Gladstone's lieutenant, was known for the best of reasons as "Harty Tarty" . . . Asquith wrote letters to his girl friend during cabinet meetings; Lloyd George regarded sex as healthy therapy and worked hard at it . . . Disraeli, before he married for money (and, to be fair, found sincere affection), put it about vigorously in co-respondent country.'

This latter charge could never be levelled against Rupert Mountjoy, for not a single married lady makes an appearance in his personal reminiscences, even though in 1906 it was strongly hinted in the Christmas issue of *The Cremorne*, a spicy Edwardian underground magazine, that Rupert was having an affair with Lady Virginia Montairy, the pretty young wife of a high-ranking officer in the Indian Army.

A sceptic might account for this fact by saying that Rupert was frightened to mention their names in his ribald memoirs, but I would like to think that, whilst Rupert hugely enjoyed penning the uninhibited lusty details of his many and varied bedroom frolics, he would indignantly insist that only a cad would reveal the names of his married *amorata*. For, unlike some of his contemporaries, he was at pains to stress that a gentleman should never force unwanted attentions upon unwilling partners. Although his desire to explore the boundaries of sexual mechanics is also expressed in this book, when during an escapade with two frolicsome waitresses at a party on the eve of the Grand National, he remarks to his cousin Beresford, that 'surely nothing which is physically possible can be unnatural.'

This fifth selection from Rupert's journal dates from Spring 1908, when he was twenty-four years old and relishing to the full the life of a wealthy young man-about-town, living (courtesy of a family friend) rent-free in fashionable Bloomsbury, in a house fully staffed by willing servants, with little to do except try out the latest amusements of the day with his close circle of friends.

As has been noted in the thumbnail sketches of Rupert Mountjoy's life in the four previous volumes of extracts from his journal, this idle sybaritic lifestyle came to an abrupt end five and a half years after the events so vividly described in this book, when he foolishly made a disastrous speculation involving the purchases of racehorses from a dishonest breeder, which left him penniless. Indeed, Rupert narrowly escaped a police prosecution after his debts were settled by his furious father, Colonel Harold Elton Fortescue Mountjoy, late of the Ninth Punjab Rifles, who afterwards banished his errant son to Australia with a one-way ticket to Sydney and (unknown to the Colonel) a handsome cheque for £2,000 from his mother.

Despite this generous gift, Rupert felt obliged to raise as much ready cash as possible before leaving England in October 1913, in order to settle some further outstanding bills, and thus instructed the fashionable Society solicitor Sir David Godfrey to see how much a French publisher would pay for the rights of his secret autobiography, since as from mid-Victorian times even up until the early 1960s, a great amount of illicit gallant literature in English was being smuggled into Britain from Paris.

Sir David was himself a man of robust sexual proclivities and a fellow member of the Cremornites Dining Society, a clique of notorious rakes which included the writer Max Dalmaine, Colonel Alan Brooke of the Grenadier Guards, the financier Sir Ronald Dunn and the appropriately named Dr Jonathan Letchmore, whose birthday party was graphically reported by Rupert in the previous volume in this series [*see* The Intimate Memoirs of an Edwardian Dandy IV: Country Matters – *Editor*].

So, instead of telegraphing his French contacts, Sir David simply sold Rupert's manuscript to the editor of the Cremornites' own saucy magazine, which was secretly printed in London, adding fifty pounds of his own money when he sent Rupert a cheque 'which you can repay when you return home'. Never on open sale, of course, copies are now very rare. A pirated edition, circulated in 1919, which was published by 'The Society of Venus and Priapus', was a cover for the Manchester printer Oswald Knuckleberry, who was forced to flee the country for South America in 1923 when police discovered thousands of erotic books and explicit nude photographs at his factory in West Didsbury.

But Rupert was never to step foot in England again, although he wrote home regularly to his parents and friends, and repaid the loan less than three months later, for only six weeks after arriving in Australia he went into partnership with one Marco Valducci, a local Italian restaurateur, and opened The Odd-Bods, an exclusive but highly raunchy gentleman's club in the heart of Sydney. The club made substantial profits, and in 1915 Rupert married a pretty heiress, Nancy du Boute, who dissuaded him from joining one of the Australian regiments which were later cut to pieces in the Dardanelles campaign during the Great War.

His travels were by no means at an end, however. In 1920, after Nancy had inherited a little over £100,000 from her late father, the Mountjoys visited a friend of the du Boute family in Southern California. Rupert was so taken with American ways and especially the excitement of the burgeoning film industry that he emigrated a second time and purchased a palatial mansion in Beverly Hills, later lived in by several Hollywood moguls until it was destroyed by a fierce forest fire in 1949. Apparently, his wife had no objection to the move, and the family (by then Nancy had produced twin boys and a girl) moved, lock, stock and barrel, to America in the following year. Rupert's interest in the movie industry soon cooled and instead he made some shrewd investments in real estate (though for a time his son Martin became a film extra and can briefly be seen with Clark Gable in *Gone With The Wind*) and he and Nancy lived quietly to a ripe old age.

There may be some who question the need to produce and receive explicit unexpurgated material, but most authorities would now accept that, within agreed wide-ranging parameters, adults should be allowed to read whatever they want. And as Dr Warwick Jackson observed in *His Mighty Engine*, an amusing though scholarly book on Edwardian erotica: 'Authors such as Rupert Mountjoy set themselves firmly against the authoritarian notion that mainstream sexuality was an area which had to be stringently controlled by the ruling Establishment, and it is timely that his writing has survived the years to be openly republished almost one hundred years later, providing an unconventional, irreverent insight into the manners and mores of a long vanished world.'

Arthur Garvice
Toronto
December, 1994

Sir Toby: Dost thou think, because thou art virtuous, there shall be no more cakes and ale?
Clown: Yes by Saint Anne: and ginger shall be hot i' the mouth too.

TWELFTH NIGHT
William Shakespeare

CHAPTER ONE

Comings and Goings

UNTIL YESTERDAY, I ALWAYS MAINTAINED that, even from the very first moments of struggling out of slumber, it was quite easy to make a judgement as to whether it was worthwhile counting up to three and then jumping out of bed and opening the curtains to greet the new day – or whether it would be best simply to turn over and surrender oneself to the joys of a final sweet sleep before a servant knocks on the door with an early morning cup of tea.

Now I realise that not everyone has the privilege of making such a choice, but frankly, until my inheritance from Uncle Humphrey runs out, I am lucky enough to be in the happy situation of being able to decide whether or not I want to leave my bed at half past eight on a brisk March morning. Certainly, this time last year I would have had no difficulty in selecting which path to follow, for in all likelihood the soft voluptuous curves of Mary, the prettiest house-maid it has ever been my pleasure to poke, would be pressed against me, and I would roll her over on to her side and position my erect throbbing prick between her luscious bum cheeks and begin the day with a grand 'doggie-style' fuck.

Alas, Mary is no longer in my employ, for she decamped along with my valet Lawbress to take up service out of town in Sussex, at the country seat of Sir Rodney and Lady Brampton. I had hoped that the housekeeper, Mrs Harrow, would have employed a similar obliging young girl, but unfortunately she has replaced Mary with Esme, a most efficient but sadly extremely plain mature woman in her late thirties whom I would pay to keep out of my bed!

Incidentally, I have not replaced Lawbress, but instead have raised the wages of Edwards, my footman, by the munificent sum of ten pounds a year, to take on additional duties as my valet. For one of my New Year resolutions was to keep my expenses within the limits set by my Uncle Humphrey when he offered me the use of this sumptuously furnished town house in Bedford Square for a further twelve months.

I should explain to those readers who have not scanned through my previous jottings that in fact I am living here courtesy not only of my uncle, but his old friend Colonel Wright, the owner of 69 Bedford Square, who went to India almost three years ago to serve as deputy chairman of the Royal Commission on Native Education and, according to Uncle Humphrey, was persuaded to stay on in Madras 'by a dusky maiden young enough to be his daughter, the lucky old devil'.

Therefore, even if I wished, it would be difficult

for me to dismiss any servant without very good cause, especially as Mrs Harrow has been in Colonel Wright's service for the past seventeen years and, as Beresford, my cousin and good chum said to me in the lounge of the Jim Jam Club [*an infamous semi-secret rendezvous in Great Windmill Street which flourished in the late Victorian and Edwardian eras. As Prince of Wales, King Edward VII was a frequent visitor to the Club, especially when raunchy cabarets featuring nude chorus girls were staged there – Editor*] when I complained about the loss of Mary's deliciously tight wet pussey: 'My dear Rupert, take it from me, getting involved with the servants always ends in tears.'

'All very well for you to say that, Berry,' I grumbled as he passed me a large whisky and soda. 'Especially as I cannot believe that you are not fucking Lizzie, that gorgeous full-bosomed girl who answers the door when I come round to your apartment in Cavendish Square.'

He flashed me a quick smile and settled himself down in a comfortable armchair. '*Touché*, old boy, but in fact I can tell you that my experience with Lizzie proved my point. I only employ servants from Aspiso's [*the top domestic service agency in London until the advent of World War One – Editor*] as there is little point in maintaining full-time staff right now, when I am able to spend only one week in four in London. Hopefully, I will be able to join you for some fine larks in town on a more permanent basis when Papa and Mama sail for America next month, for a long vacation with sister Maud, now Mrs Henry G. Fairweather of

536 Fifth Avenue, New York City.

'Anyhow, be that as it may, I won't deny that my shaft automatically stiffened at the sight of young Lizzie's luscious figure. Once or twice, I could have sworn that she deliberately bent down and picked up imaginary particles of dust from the carpet with the top buttons of her blouse undone so that I had a bird's eye view of the swell of her breasts, and as I was leaving the apartment on this particular morning in question, I noticed that she brushed by me rather closer than necessary in the narrow space in the hall between the wall and the grandfather clock. I went down to play tennis at my club, but my enjoyment of a damned good game with our mutual friend Richard Mabb was marred when an attendant informed me that the boiler had suddenly packed up, and so there was no hot water available for a shower.

'When I returned home, I filled the bath with lashings of hot water, stripped off my tennis togs, plunged in and washed off all the grime and perspiration.'

I could not resist interrupting him to ask, 'And I suppose you still sing in the bath, Berry, for there were reports in the newspapers last week that Sir Arthur Sullivan is turning in his grave.'

'Ha, ha, very funny, Rupert,' he replied, swigging down his cognac. 'Anyhow, at this point I suddenly realised that in my haste I had forgotten to check whether Lizzie had put out any fresh towels since my earlier ablutions before breakfast, and I groaned when I saw that the rail was bare. So, after I had pulled out the plug, I hauled myself out of the bath and padded out into the hall to retrieve a warm towel from the linen cupboard.

'The door was already slightly ajar and when I pulled it completely open – well, I don't know who was more surprised, myself or Lizzie, who stood there open-mouthed with the linen basket, looking up and down my naked wet body. I hastily cupped a hand over my groin and gasped, 'Oh, I do beg your pardon, Lizzie, but there aren't any towels in the bathroom.'

' "That's all right, sir, no harm done," she said brightly. "Here, let me give you a nice clean one before you catch your death of cold." With that pert remark, the pretty little minx threw a towel at me in such a way that I was forced to use both hands to catch it, and thus exposed my naked cock and balls to her interested gaze. Nevertheless, I draped the towel around my waist and Lizzie passed me another one, with which I dried my face, then turned aside and began to towel my back with some vigour. Then, to my utter astonishment, I heard Lizzie breathe softly into my ear, "There's no need to be so shy, Beresford. I've seen you staring at my titties. No, please don't apologise, I know how much you fancy fucking me – but have you ever thought that I might have been thinking along the very same lines?"

'I was so dumbfounded by this forthright declaration that I was lost for words. I turned round to face her and she undid the simple knot

13

which held up my towel. It slid swiftly to the carpet. Lizzie's eyes brightened when she looked down at my prick and she reached out, gently squeezed my balls and murmured, ''What a fine looking truncheon, but, dear me, it looks so doleful dangling so limply over your balls. Let me see if I can coax it up to attention.''

'She swiftly shrugged off her clothes and stood before me bare-breasted in a coquettish pose, wearing only a tightly fitting pair of white cotton drawers through which I could see the hairy outlines of her muff. But it was on Lizzie's creamy high-tilted breasts with their proudly erect red-topped nipples that I focused my attention. I gulped hard, for it was truly difficult to believe that this was not a dream. I shut my eyes for a moment, only to feel Lizzie's soft hands sliding down my chest and tummy, and when I opened them again she was kneeling in front of me, kissing and sucking my thickening cock, whilst her busy hands drew back my foreskin and started to rub my fast-hardening chopper.

'A delicious stab of desire shuddered through me as she lustily sucked my swollen shaft up to a full erection, teasing my knob against the roof of her mouth with her tongue, and in no time at all I felt the surge of an impending spend course through my throbbing tadger. Lizzie sensed this and took her sweet lips away for a moment before returning to the attack, somehow cramming my entire nine inches between her lips until it surely must have been touching the back of her throat. Then she began to suck noisily on my bursting tool, bobbing her head to and fro, whilst playing with my balls, gently squeezing them through the hairy bag of wrinkled pink skin.

' "Oh my God, I'm going to come if you don't stop!" I panted, and for a second time she took my pulsing prick out of her mouth. Still keeping a tight hold on my cock, she whispered, "Lie down on your back – I will ride a St George upon you."

'I obeyed without the slightest demur and lay flat on the carpet, my rampant cock sticking up like a fleshy flagpole whilst Lizzie turned her peachy rounded bum cheeks towards me and straddled my belly. With a fervent sigh, she lowered herself on my cock, remaining almost motionless for a few moments whilst we mutually enjoyed the sensation of my big cock filling her narrow love channel to the full. Then she began to rock up and down on my rigid rod, ramming herself up and down and squeezing her cuntal muscles so cleverly that I was swiftly transported to the seventh heaven of delight. My excitement soon overflowed and she moved her hips faster and faster, her delicious cunney gripping and releasing my shaft so exquisitely that, alas, I could not wait until she achieved her spend and I spurted a fountain of sticky seed, shooting up into the furthest recesses of her sopping honeypot, completely filling her love channel as jets of jism flooded out of my cock and dribbled down her inner thighs. To my great regret, Lizzie had several domestic duties to perform and I had an appointment with Doctor Jonathan Letchmore in Harley Street, so it was not possible for me to finish her off. However, I did my duty later that day and fucked the arse off her after dinner.'

I swallowed down the rest of my whisky and soda and handed my glass back for Beresford to refill. 'Why did you have to see Johnny Letchmore?' I asked my cousin, trying hard to keep a sour note out of my voice, for it had been a full ten days since I had enjoyed a fuck, and his randy story reminded me of how frustrated I was feeling about not having Mary's juicy wet pussey available whilst my long-time girl friend Diana Wigmore was studying art at the Sorbonne in Paris. 'One presumes that your cock is not going to drop off through over-use, although I dare say that Lady Angela Dickler might add that the sooner your balls were removed the better, if there were any justice in the world.'

Beresford had the grace to blush at this, for it was common knowledge at the Jim Jam Club that, whilst staying as Lady Dickler's guest at her country seat down near Crawley, his hostess had found him fucking Lady Estella Heton, one of her closest friends, when he should have been warming her bed in the prolonged absence of Lord Dickler, who himself was happily poking a wide selection of delectable Eurasian girls whilst engaged in diplomatic business on behalf of Her Britannic Majesty's Government in Singapore.

'Yes, well there is no hiding the fact that I am now *persona non grata* at Dickler Lodge,' said Beresford with a rueful sigh. 'But hopefully I can persuade Lady Angela to forgive and forget – when all is said and done, she was only sharing me with her best friend. It wasn't as if I was fucking any other of the guests.'

'Quite true, old man,' I agreed as he refilled my glass and passed it back to me. 'However, according to Lady Angela's personal secretary, you were also seen being sucked off by a seventeen-year-old scullery maid whilst you had your head between the thighs of her twin sister and were so busy bringing her off with your tongue that you were unaware of being watched.'

His face darkened as I repeated this story, which had been related to me only the day before, by Lieutenant Andrew Coles of the Horse Guards, another old chum from Varsity days who spent most of his free time at the Club.

'Mere servants' gossip. Surely I need hardly tell you how unreliable that can be. For a start, the girls were sisters, not twins, and one was eighteen and the other twenty-one,' muttered Beresford into his cognac as he rose from his chair. 'Er, isn't that the famous racehorse owner, Sir Loring Sayers? Excuse me for a moment, Rupert, I want to have a few words with him about which nag he believes has a good chance in the Grand National on Saturday week.'

He left me feeling even more depressed and wishing that I had not arranged to meet him for a midday drink, but instead stayed in bed till ten o'clock and then spent the rest of the morning catching up with my correspondence. My gloom was deepened when I watched my cousin go out of the lounge with Sir Loring and two attractive girls who looked as though they had come to the

Club directly from Madame Rosalie's establishment across the street. [*Madame Rosalie's was one of the most exclusive bordellos in Edwardian London, and catered solely for a high-class 'invitation only' clientele. Rumoured to be among its patrons were David Lloyd-George, George Bernard Shaw and several European Ambassadors – Editor.*] If my assessment of the girls was accurate, then Sir Loring and Beresford were going up to one of the private rooms on the second floor, and it would be doubtful if the lucky so-and-sos would emerge till tea-time. Whilst I realised it was foolish and wrong to be jealous of Beresford's impending fucking session, I could not help feeling somewhat envious of the fact that my cousin had pussey to spare, whilst I would have to make do with what, according to Lieutenant Coles, is known in the Armed Services as 'a five-knuckle shuffle'.

Ah well, to him that hath shall more be given, and surely my luck must change shortly, I thought to myself as I scribbled a note to him, saying that I was going to take an early light luncheon in the Club restaurant and then go for a stroll in Hyde Park before returning home in good time to dress for dinner at the Mayfair home of the American cinematographer, Mr Frederick Nolan, who had recently returned to Britain from a visit to California. This gentleman had become a firm friend since our first meeting back in '98 at my family home, Albion Towers, near the sleepy little Yorkshire village of Wharton on the edge of Knaresborough Forest [*see* An Edwardian Dandy

I: Youthful Scandals – *Editor*], and I was very much looking forward to seeing him again.

In fact, Mr Nolan was giving this dinner in honour of the famous music hall singer, Miss Maisie Macnamara, who was attracting such attention from the stage door johnnies every night after her 'house full' performances at the Empire Theatre in Leicester Square, and I hoped it would be a jolly affair. On the other hand, it was highly unlikely that I would find a partner to share my lonely bed at Mr Nolan's dinner, so I relapsed into a state of gloom until luncheon, when the chap who had passed on the juicy piece of gossip about Beresford rogering two young sisters, Lieutenant Andrew Coles of the Guards, came up and sat down at my table, as I tucked into a plate of Fillets of Plaice with Tartare Sauce and Fried Potatoes.

'Hello there, Rupert. You look like a chap who has lost a sovereign and found a sixpence,' said Andrew sympathetically. 'What's causing you to look so down in the dumps?'

'Nothing in particular, Andy. I'm simply suffering from night starvation,' I replied with a small smile, and when he furrowed his brow and said that he was unaware of this disease, I went on to explain that the condition could be easily cured by a large dose of warm, wet cunnies!

'Well, that shouldn't prove too difficult a prescription for a cocksman of your calibre,' grunted the good-looking Guards officer, pulling a large brown envelope out of his jacket pocket. Opening the envelope, he took out a couple of hand-tinted colour photographs. 'Perhaps you would like me to effect an introduction to this girl? Before you ask, the lovely lady in question is Claudia Renouvin, a French chorus girl who is currently living with Bernard Barnes at his house in St John's Wood. [*Sir Bernard Barnes (1867-1918) was a high-ranking Foreign Office official and an indefatigable collector of erotica, second only to H. Spencer Ashbee and Lord Peter Cotton – Editor*] When Bernard decided to take up photography seriously, he asked Claudia to pose for him and these are the results. I think you might find them of interest.'

He passed me the photographs and, despite myself, I drew in a sharp breath as I looked at the print of a well-proportioned nude girl kneeling on a chaise longue, pushing out her saucy bum cheeks towards the camera, a salacious smile on her enticingly pretty face.

'Not a bad picture, is it?' leered Andy, nudging me in the ribs. 'Look at the cheeky little cat – she seems to be saying how much she would like a good thick stiffie pushed in between those lovely bum cheeks. Mind, she looks even tastier from the front,' he added as I peered at the second photograph, which showed the still naked Claudia facing the camera and leaning back against a whitewashed wall. There was no doubt that she was a perfect specimen of feminine pulchritude, possessing a face distinguished by fine cheekbones, a full, voluptuous mouth and an abundance of soft chestnut hair. The photograph showed her brushing the soft tresses away from her delightful features with her hands. Her plump young breasts were topped with berry-like erect nipples and her flat belly led down to superbly formed thighs, as sweet as any sculptor might have fashioned, the calves and ankles slender and the thighs fulsome. And between her thighs, at the base of her belly, lay a glossy abundance of light brown curls that frothed all about her mount, and I could clearly see the shell-like lips of her cunney pouting out. And as I gazed upon this sultry magnificent goddess of desire, my cock thickened and rose up in salute to her.

'My God, this is too much,' I murmured, gaping at a third photograph, which showed Claudia with her fingers sliding inside that exquisite fluffy muff. The tip of her index finger was dipped inside her cunney and her eyes were closed as if she were already in a self-induced trance of ecstasy.

I handed the photographs back to Andy and used a table napkin to wipe my brow, saying, 'Thanks, but I'm afraid they haven't cheered me up. To be frank, now I feel even more gloomy. Not only am I reminded how desperate I am for a large helping of pussey-pie, but I'm also feeling extremely jealous of old Sir Bernard. I mean, I know he is a randy old so-and-so, but he must be well over eighty by now and surely he can't still be capable of giving this lovely girl a good poke.'

'Don't you believe it, old boy,' said the good-looking Guards officer cheerily as he heaved himself out of his chair. 'There's many a good tune played on an old fiddle, as Bernard would tell you himself, except that he's out of the country, taking the waters in Baden Baden. Anyhow, for what it is worth, my advice is to stop moping and take yourself off over the road for a swift shag at Madame Rosalie's. See if you can fix yourself up with Conchita, that new Spanish girl from Barcelona who is staying with Rosalie for a few weeks before she goes off to Mexico. I can't give you a personal recommendation, but after seeing how superbly she sucked off Major Parsifal a few days ago at a rather wild party in the mess, I'm sure you won't be disappointed.'

I nodded, and spoke with a fresh lightness in my voice: 'A most sensible suggestion, Lieutenant Coles, for which you will be duly mentioned in dispatches. As you rightly say, there's no time like the present. I'll go over to Madame Rosalie's right now and spend the afternoon with Conchita or some other frisky little filly.'

Andy Coles shook his head sadly. 'Sorry, Rupert, you'll have to wait till tomorrow. I'd rather fancied a fuck myself this afternoon, but when I telephoned half an hour ago, Rosalie told me that all the girls are out working for the rest of the day. In fact, two of her best girls are here right now in one of the *salles privées* with Sir Loring Sayers and your cousin Beresford. Still, if you are feeling really desperate, you could always ask to join in. But if Sir Loring isn't in the mood for sharing, how about joining me and some of the other chaps for a session of billiards in the games room?'

'Thank you, Andy, I might well take up that invitation,' I replied, and he called back, 'Good show. We'll look forward to seeing you.' Then he slipped the photographs of the gorgeous Claudia back into his jacket and made his way towards the door.

A waiter came over and as I was ordering a coffee and a small glass of cognac I suddenly remembered that I had not yet read more than the opening paragraph of the letter I had received in the afternoon post yesterday. [*An Edwardian Londoner could expect at least three daily deliveries of mail – Editor*] from Lady Amber Berlynne, the ravishing eighteen-year-old nymph with whom I had enjoyed some wonderful romps in Torbay the previous summer [*see* An Edwardian Dandy IV: Country Matters – *Editor*]. Amber was spending the Spring with her parents at their delightful country estate between Chester and Aldford, and my suspicions that the joys of the quiet rural life were beginning to pall for this lively lass were proved correct when I settled down to peruse her long letter in earnest, which read as follows:

Darling Rupert,

I blush with shame when I recall that one of my New Year resolutions was to answer my correspondence more promptly. It must be at least a full month since I received your nice gossipy letter with all the news and views about the people you meet in London, whom I can only read about in the weekly illustrated journals. Do forgive me and keep writing for I so enjoy hearing from you – if nothing else, your letters remind me of the fun and games we had together at Penny Maltin's down in Devon last summer!

Life has been rather dreary up here until a fortnight or so ago, when Mama arranged for me to travel to Chester and sit for Mr Eric Marks the portrait painter, who is staying there with his brother until he goes to France for the summer. I had not really wanted to go, but Mama was so impressed with Mr Marks' picture of Estelle, Lady Vincent's eldest daughter, that she promptly commissioned him to paint me. And when I told her I was hardly overjoyed at the prospect of spending long boring afternoons in Mr Marks' studio, she replied that Estelle had enjoyed the experience and she saw no reason why I should not do the same.

'Lady Vincent informs me that Mr Marks is a very pleasant gentleman,' said Mama in a voice which brooked no argument. 'He is coming to take tea with us on Thursday, when he can make a few preliminary sketches of you before starting work in his studio. Amber, I apologise for the short notice, but I am afraid you must cancel any other arrangements you may have made as this is the only time that Mr Marks is free to see you.'

Now, as it happened, I had made no plans for Thursday afternoon – although I grumbled about the inconvenience of having to contact several friends who would be disappointed that I was now unable to spend the day with them before I gave Mama my word that I would be present for tea that day as she had requested. Nevertheless, when the time came to meet Mr Marks, I was feeling somewhat out-of-sorts, for I was still dubious about the idea of having my picture painted, but then Smithers announced that Mr Marks had arrived and Mama instructed the butler to show him in.

However, I was pleasantly surprised to discover that he was a handsome broad-shouldered gentleman in his early thirties. His easy manner and good humour put me at ease almost immediately, and I could well see why (as Estelle Vincent was later to tell me, when I saw her some time afterwards) so many of Mr Marks' models fell for his undoubted charm, and finished up in bed with the talented artist.

After tea, Mama gave him permission to make some preliminary sketches of me in the drawing-room and we arranged that I should go to Chester the following Monday for my first sitting. His studio is in Grosvenor Street, so our housekeeper Mrs Attlee, who was to act as my chaperone, could visit the City Museum whilst Eric (for we soon dispensed with unnecessary formalities) began his work.

I had been very naughty for, unknown to Mama, I had packed a complete change of clothes for the occasion, into which I changed in Eric's bedroom. I divested myself completely of my clothes and stood naked for a few moments, admiring my firm breasts and fluffy flaxen bush, before slipping on a camisole fashioned from the softest Irish linen, trimmed with lace, through which the generous swell of my breasts and long pointy nipples were plainly visible, and a pair of close-fitting knickers made from the same sheer fabric, which showed the contours of my tight curvy bum behind and the thick thatch of pussey hair in front, and I finished by putting on my best white silk stockings held up by frilly baby-blue satin garters.

I cupped the full roundness of my bosoms in my

hands and my sensitive nipples, ever mobile to the merest touch, as you well know, swelled and hardened in a manner which I recall you sweetly told me was reminiscent of pink buds adorning certain varieties of miniature roses. Then, checking my reflection in the mirror, it occurred to me what a great shame it would be to hide these sensual underclothes under a dress, even one as pretty as the fine cotton gown designed by Monsieur Arglenis in Paris, which I had deliberately chosen for its low-cut bodice that revealed such a daring expanse of cleavage. It was doubtful that Eric would complain, even if I tripped into the studio half-naked with my bare breasts bouncing up and down and luscious bottom cheeks jiggling enticingly inside my taut white knickers. With this lascivious thought in mind, I opened the door. Eric drew in a sharp breath as I moved across to take up my position, reclining gracefully along the length of a well-padded settee, and tugging down my bodice to show off even more of my generous bosom as I sat down.

'You look truly magnificent,' Eric said, picking up a large stick of charcoal. 'Now make yourself comfortable and we'll begin.'

For an hour or so, I sat stock-still as Eric worked assiduously, but then he threw down his charcoal pencil and groaned, 'It's no good, I can't carry on like this – Amber, I'm dreadfully sorry, but I shall have to begin again and this time I must ask you to change into a winter outfit.'

'But why, Eric?' I asked with as innocent a voice as I could muster. 'My friends all say that this dress really suits me.'

'It does, my dear girl,' he replied huskily. 'Only I am

26

finding it extremely difficult to concentrate on your face when my eyes keep finding themselves riveted to your exquisite figure – which must be covered up or I will be unable to complete your picture.'

'Oh, then it is I who should apologise for wearing a costume which has disturbed your concentration,' I exclaimed, and then I added thoughtfully, 'On the other hand, Eric, I don't think it would solve the problem if I simply changed into less revealing clothes, for surely you would still be left wondering how I looked au naturel.'

His eyes brightened. He did not reply, but came over to sit down next to me. Then he cleared his throat and slid his arm around my waist and muttered hoarsely in my ear, 'Monsieur Toulouse-Lautrec always maintained that an artist could only capture the essential spirit of a pretty model if he first made love to her.'

'Did he now?' I rejoined with a giggle, feeling a delicious tingling sensation spreading out from my pussey. 'Well, I don't know how much truth there is in his maxim, but I have a feeling that I am going to find out.'

Eric smiled and, gently pushing me down upon my back, he kissed me and I found myself responding, sliding my tongue between his teeth as his tongue probed in my open mouth, and then I felt his hand fondling my breasts and my senses began to dance. Tearing my lips away from his passionate kiss, I gasped, 'Wait a minute, I don't want to crease these clothes, I'll take them off now.'

I undressed quickly and, in no time at all, stood in front of him in the nude. With a cheeky grin, I said, 'There you are, sir. Now the goods are on display, you

27

had better make your purchase or I will have to wrap everything up again.'

'Oh, have no fear, I shall buy everything on offer! My only problem will be not to spend too much too quickly!' he retorted wittily, and pulled me down to sit on his lap. 'I've been willing this moment from the very first moment I saw you.'

He slipped his hands underneath my breasts, pressing them together and showering them with kisses, and as he buried his face in the soft, yielding flesh, savouring the delicate aroma of warm, scented skin, he breathed, 'Amber, your breasts are magnificent and I must pay due homage to these two divine beauties.'

'Be my guest,' I murmured, whereupon Eric lunged at one engorged red tittie, nipping it lightly with his teeth and then sucking it, deep and long. Barely pausing, he squeezed my breasts together until my nipples almost touched (which always sends an erotic shiver through my body) and then, licking his lips, he took them both in his mouth simultaneously, nibbling and flicking each engorged cherry with his tongue before sucking them in a strong, powerful rhythm which caused me to groan with delight.

My blood was now up and, climbing from his lap, my cheeks flushed, my breasts sheened with a mix of perspiration and saliva, I rapidly undid the buttons of his fly and out sprang his huge bursting stalk, which was quite beautifully formed and well ornamented by a large pair of tight looking balls. However, I was loath to break my rule of never making love on a first meeting, and I was also concerned that Mrs Attlee might decide to come up to the studio to see how Eric's picture was progressing. So I decided only to give a tit-fuck to the randy artist, who swiftly pulled off his clothes when I asked him to undress so that I could enjoy the sight of his manly frame. Eric is a well-built chap with broad shoulders and a deep chest covered with a mass of dark curly hair, but it was his thick cock which interested me most as it stood majestically upright between his thighs.

With genuine regret, I explained why a full fuck would have to wait for more auspicious circumstances, and to his credit he did not try and force me to change my mind (not that I would have done), unlike some foolish young men of my acquaintance. Then I knelt down in front of him and, taking hold of his blue-veined tool, I briskly rubbed my hand up and down his smooth hot shaft, from his balls up to the tip of his knob, before gently kissing the ruby helmet. With my other hand, I pressed my bosoms together and slid his huge throbbing truncheon in the cleft between my heavy, moist tits.

'Now then, Eric, cream my titties with your jism,' I urged him, wrapping my fingers even more tightly around his cock, and I fisted my hand at a great pace up and down his palpitating prick.

No man has managed to hold back for more than a minute of this bosomy massage and, sure enough, Eric soon moaned as, in a tumultuous climax, he let fly a tremendous fountain of frothy seed which sprayed a white necklace of spunk across my titties. I leaned further forward to rub his jerking cock up and down the cleft, smearing the jism all around my saucer-shaped aureoles. Then I pressed my breasts even closer around his still stiff shaft and he cried out in ecstasy, spurting the remnants of his spend on to my chin.

He lay back on the settee, exhausted from this thrilling little sexual exercise. His cock slowly began to droop and hang limply downwards. But he watched with an expression of pure pleasure whilst I sensuously massaged my breasts and elongated nipples with his warm spunk until they gleamed wetly in the Spring sunlight, and smiled as I languourously licked each finger in turn, savouring the salty tang upon my lips and tongue.

We dressed ourselves and I resumed my modelling position on the settee, whilst Eric picked up his pencil and went back to work with a flourish. Now, although this next piece of information will hardly distress you, I doubt if I will ever find out whether Eric is good at either poking or painting because the very next day Eric received a telegram from none other than Mrs Keppel [King Edward VII's most favoured mistress – Editor] asking him to return to London to paint her daughter, who would only be free to sit in the coming three weeks, and so we have been forced to postpone further sittings until the autumn.

Of course I am always pleased to see you, dear Rupert, but especially so just now, for I have not had a proper fuck for ages and, indeed, I was so tired of using my dildo that, quite candidly, I was almost prepared to let Eric Marks fuck me despite my strict adherence to my aforesaid rule of not letting a man poke me until well into the relationship.

Now I have some further news which I do hope will be of interest to you. An American friend of my parents, Mr Foxhall Keene, has unexpectedly arrived from New York today and is making up a party to travel up to Aintree on Friday week to see his two horses, Chorus and Prophet III, run in the Grand National steeplechase. I have been invited to join the party and

30

Mr Keene has kindly written asking if I would like to invite a partner. We will be staying on in Liverpool on Saturday night for a dinner and ball at the Adelphi Hotel, where rooms have been reserved for us. Of course, it is too late for you to book a room there, but I am sure that a generous tip to the porter will ensure that you are able to slip upstairs after the party and spend the night in my bed.

Do say you'll come, darling, we'll have a grand time. Let me know as soon as possible if you're free. Since last month, we now have the luxury of a telephone – and would you believe that our number is Aldford 69! My poor Mama could not understand why I laughed out loud when she informed me of the number nor why I remarked that it was a most appropriate number as far as I was concerned.
All my love,
Amber

I gnawed my lower lip as I folded her letter and put it back inside the envelope. As luck would have it, my only engagement for that weekend was to dine at my Aunt Agatha's on Friday night, and hopefully I could square Beresford to go in my place if my bowing from my Aunt's dinner party disturbed her table arrangements.

So, feeling far better after reading this lovely letter, I trotted down to the Club offices and asked the telephonist to try and connect me with Amber's telephone number at six o'clock that evening. Meanwhile, I scribbled out a short telegram of acceptance, in case she was not at home, and decided to ask Beresford as soon as possible if he would kindly dine at Aunt Agatha's on Saturday week.

By now, I guessed that he and Sir Loring would have had their wicked way with the two girls from Madame Rosalie's, so I took the elevator up to the *salles privées* on the third floor, where a flunkey informed me that Sir Loring had booked room 12 for the afternoon. I marched through the corridor to the door, but just as I raised my hand to knock, the door opened and Sir Loring himself appeared, clad in a red silk dressing-gown.

'Hello there, young Rupert, what brings you here?' the baronet asked genially. 'Come on in, my boy. I heard your footsteps in the corridor and thought Grey might at last be coming up with the two bottles of champagne I ordered fifteen minutes ago. I don't want to complain to the committee, but the old boy's getting slower and slower and the Club should really pension him off. Where the devil can he have got to?'

Fortunately for Grey, he shuffled round the corner with a loaded tray just at that very moment, and I stood aside to let him through.

'I'm sorry to have taken so long,' puffed the old retainer, 'but we didn't have any '02 Piper Heidsieck on ice, so I've brought up two bottles of '03 Louis Roederer, which I hope will be satisfactory.'

'Yes, yes, that will do well enough,' said Sir Loring, fishing out a sovereign from his pocket whilst we followed the waiter into the room, where he set down the tray on a table.

'Here you are, Grey – you may keep the

change,' Sir Loring added, and Grey thanked him profusely, then went out, shutting the door firmly behind him. 'Well, now, at last we have something to drink. Oh, but I had better first introduce you to two charming young ladies. Rupert, meet Becky and Dora. Girls, this gentleman is Rupert Mountjoy, Beresford's cousin.'

The two pretty girls, one auburn-haired and the other a strawberry blonde, were sitting up together, bare-breasted in the large double bed, their arms entwined around each other.

'Pleased to meet you, Rupert. I'm Becky, and this is my sister Dora,' said the attractive little minx whose long tresses of glossy, copper-coloured hair tumbled over her shoulders. She winked at me cheekily and went on, 'Now, I've just enjoyed a nice long fuck with your cousin and I must say that he is a very good pussey-eater – does this trait run in the family?'

'Of course it does, and I taught him all he knows,' I answered with a smile, and was rewarded with a burst of giggling from both girls. 'In fact, I have an important message for Beresford. Surely he has not already made his leave from such delightful company?'

'No, he's just gone to the bathroom and will be out shortly,' said Sir Loring, popping the cork on one of the bottles and pouring out some champagne. 'Here, Rupert, help yourself to some fizz, and there are some sandwiches left from our luncheon if you're hungry. Stay where you are, ladies – I'll bring your glasses over to you,' he

added as Beresford came back from the bathroom, also dressed in one of the smart silk robes
which the Jim Jam Club provide for those
members using the facilities of the *salles privées*.

'Hello, Rupert,' said my cousin, sitting on the
bed and kissing Becky on the cheek, before
adding with a wicked grin, 'I can guess what
brings you up here, old boy.'

I shook my head. 'I doubt it, Berry. You might
not believe this, but I'm only here to ask whether
you'll be good enough to take my place and dine
at Aunt Agatha's on Friday week as I have been
invited to go to Aintree and see the Grand
National.'

Beresford threw up his arms, saying, 'What a
coincidence! I'm sorry, cousin, but I can't help
you. As a matter of fact, Sir Loring and I are also
off to see the big race.'

'Yes, and you're going to take us with you,
aren't you?' chimed in Dora, and Sir Loring gave
a gruff chuckle. 'Indeed we are, my dear.
Unfortunately, I've had to scratch my own
National entry, Hammersmith's Folly. He bruised
a fetlock rather badly last week, so I thought I'd
make up for the disappointment by watching the
race with two game little fillies instead.'

We drank a bumper to the swift recovery of
Hammersmith's Folly, and then Sir Loring,
Beresford and myself toasted the girls and they
responded in kind. We finished off the vintage
champagne and I must admit that by about three
o'clock the five of us, if not three sheets to the
wind, were all feeling extremely merry. Sir Loring

and Beresford had by now slipped off their robes and were lying in bed with the girls, but poor Sir Loring, who had also quaffed half a bottle of brandy before Grey arrived with the champagne, was very soon deep in the Land of Nod. I sat in an easy chair, exchanging gossip about various mutual friends.

Suddenly Becky frowned and wagged a finger at me. 'Why are you still wearing your clothes, Rupert?' she scolded, then she sat up and exposed her full creamy breasts with their large tawney titties. 'Take them off this minute, you silly boy! It isn't at all cold in here.'

Dora let out a lascivious cackle and exclaimed, 'Yes, Rupert, do as she says – because Becky and I have a small wager as to whether you have a bigger cock than your cousin. A sovereign, wasn't it, Becky?'

'That's right, and to make the bet even more interesting, whoever has the largest tadger can fuck me,' said her sister grandly. 'So come on, gentlemen, let us see which of you has most to offer.'

The promise of a fuck meant that neither Beresford nor myself needed any further bidding, and the girls pushed my cousin out of bed whilst I swiftly pulled off my clothes. We stood side by side, but perhaps it was a mix of our natural shyness and the copious amount of champagne we had drunk, for neither of us could achieve a stiffie and our cocks dangled limply between our thighs.

Dora smoothed a hand over her chin and

said thoughtfully, 'Well, they look about the same to me, but I would dearly like to see what those sizeable weapons look like once they are primed.'

'So would I,' agreed Becky thoughtfully. 'Now what can we do to stiffen up their cocks? Oh, I know – let's tan their hides!'

'What a splendid idea, darling,' chirped Dora as she swung herself out of the bed. 'Who'll be first? Well, you're nearest, Beresford. Bend down, sir, and touch your toes.'

'Very well, miss,' said my cousin, and he obeyed her command, opening his legs slightly so that the girls could see his hanging ballsack. Dora passed her hand lightly across his bare buttocks and then she nodded to Becky, who delivered the first slap on his arse with the palm of her hand. The girls smacked his behind in turn and his dimpled bum cheeks were soon quite rosy in colour from this sweet spanking.

'There, you naughty fellow. How dare you come to us with a limp prick?' chided Becky, delivering a resounding whack on Beresford's bottom.

'Such an impudent fellow! There, take that!' Dora panted, as she delivered another mighty wallop, which caused him to yelp, 'Hey, steady on! Enough's enough, you know!'

I craned my head forward and observed that this chastisement had caused a most perceptible swelling of Beresford's shaft, which now stood up against his belly in a rampant state of erection. Then I looked down and saw that my own prick had also hardened to its fullest height and was standing up majestically, the uncapped knob touching my navel.

'My, look at that, Dora,' cried Becky with delight. 'We've two fine thick specimens here, to be sure. But which is the biggest, that is the question?'

She looked critically at our cocks and then turned to Dora and giggled, 'I wouldn't have thought there could be more than a half-inch difference between the pair of them. Let's call it a tie and cancel our bet! But you choose which cock you would like to be fucked with, for it was your idea to play this jolly game.'

'Thank you, Becky darling, you're very kind,' said Dora, and she grabbed hold of Beresford's cock and chuckled. 'Well, since it was your poor bum which took the beating, you can have the first fuck. You have no objections, I presume.'

'None whatsoever,' responded Beresford, and he grabbed hold of the saucy girl and after a passionate preliminary embrace they sank down on the carpet (for it would have been an act of cruelty to wake Sir Loring, who was sleeping so peacefully) and Dora stretched herself out whilst I took a pillow from the bed and slipped it under her head. She really was a most seductive creature, with extremely large breasts, high-tipped pointed titties. Her mound was lightly covered with a profusion of downy brown hair, which somehow made the glowing chink between the pouting lips of her cunney even more inviting.

Beresford took a deep breath and blew out his

cheeks, expelling the air from his lungs as he took his rock-hard cock in his hand. Then, as he knelt in front of Dora, he drew back his foreskin, making his purple helmet bound and swell in his palm. Then he carefully laid himself down on top of her soft curvaceous body and they exchanged a burning kiss whilst my cousin slid his hand round the trembling girl's exquisite muff of pussey hair, slipping his index finger into her moistening quim, which readily opened to his gentle yet persistent touch. He dipped first the one and then a second and then a third finger in and out of her cunney, rubbing the knuckle of his thumb against her clitty which made Dora squirm with delight. She parted her legs to await the entrance of his prick into her yearning cunt, but Becky could see that, although the uncapped mauve knob was placed between Dora's thighs, Beresford was having difficulty in entering her love funnel, despite the ample flowing of cuntal juices from Dora's pussey.

Beresford drew back to wet his knob, but Becky now stepped forward and knelt down beside the couple, murmuring kindly, 'Here, let me help you. Dora has such a tight little cunt that a boy like you with such a big cock has to be very gentle with her.'

She took his throbbing tool in her hand and washed his domed bell-end with her tongue. Then she lifted her head and, holding his palpitating prick in one hand, she opened Dora's love lips with the other and guided his quivering cock between them until it was well lodged

38

within the portals of her tight, clinging cunney. Slowly he started to fuck her, sliding his shaft in and out of her juicy love box, and soon the couple were rocking furiously as he pounded his thick prick into her willing cunt.

'Ooooh! Ooooh! That's the ticket!' panted Dora and she slid her hands down Beresford's back to grasp his bum cheeks, pulling him even deeper inside her, and lifting her hips to welcome the thrusts of his throbbing tool inside her sopping snatch. 'Now, Berry, now! Shoot your spunk, you big cocked boy!' she cried out, and my cousin duly obliged her, increasing the speed of his heaving and bucking until, with short, stabbing strokes, he shot a creamy stream of seed into her tingling cunt. At the same time, Dora herself began her journey to paradise, shuddering as the warm waves of a glorious climax crashed through her entire body.

The sight of this erotic frolic had stimulated Becky and I to boiling point and now the gorgeous girl embraced me passionately as we stood belly to belly, my pulsing stiff cock squeezed deliciously between our tummies.

'Come round to the other side of the bed,' she whispered, taking a second pillow from the bed where Sir Loring lay, still deep in the arms of Morpheus. And then she lay down on the luxurious Persian carpet with her thighs parted, and let her fingers stray inside the thatch of glossy auburn pussey hair, tweaking open her cunney lips with the tip of her forefinger. 'Now for the moment of truth, Rupert. Can you bring me off with your tongue as nicely as your cousin? Remember, you told me that you taught him everything he knows!'

'Your wish is my command,' I said gallantly and without further ado I positioned myself on my stomach between her legs, placing one hand under her fleshy bottom to provide further elevation and the other on her mound to spread her pussey lips with my thumb and middle finger.

How beautiful Becky looked lying there, her creamy breasts capped by nut-brown nipples which were already proudly jutting out in anticipation of our impending fuck. Her lustrous triangle of pussey hair was more inviting to my hungry lips than a dish of the rarest, most expensive delicacies from any of the finest French restaurants in London.

I started by kissing her rubbery erect titties, before sliding my face down to the cleft between her thighs, inhaling with genuine pleasure the delicate cuntal aroma as I placed my lips over her swollen clitty and sucked it into my mouth, where the tip of my tongue began to explore it from all directions.

'M'mm, that's quite wonderful Rupert,' murmured Becky, throwing her legs around my back and letting out a joyous little yelp when I found the base of her clitty and began twirling my tongue around it. As I flicked it up and down, she became more and more excited and when I paused for a moment to draw breath, with a saucy giggle she turned over to lie on her belly, immediately raising her pert chubby backside whilst I ran my tongue down the ridge of her spine. I clutched her buttocks and pulled them apart, kneading the jouncy globes in my hands whilst she ducked her head and wriggled her saucy bum cheeks from side to side.

'Please bring me off with your tongue,' she gasped, raising the ripe orbs of her delicious bottom even higher so that I could lick the wrinkled little rear dimple which winked so receptively to my touch and then along the secret pathway between her bum-hole and cunney, twisting round to lie on my back, I slid my face under her.

My mouth was soon buried in Becky's dense, damp bush and my tongue tracked through her enveloping hirsute jungle to seek out her already open and welcoming cunney lips, and then her engorged stiff clitty which was equally receptive to my attentions. Her hips rose and fell as a series of orgasmic spasms sped through her body and a gush of tangy love juice filled my mouth, which I swallowed, struggling to hold her still in the repeated surges until they slowly subsided.

'Oh, Rupert, that was a truly divine spend,' exclaimed Becky as she turned herself round and straddled me. 'Now I can hardly wait to feel the whole of your thick prick throbbing inside my cunt!'

'Nor can I, my dear,' I grinned as Becky lowered her sopping pussey slowly on to the ruby helmet of my swollen shaft, and I must say that it was extraordinarily stimulating to see inch after inch of my blue-veined column disappear into her juicy crack. She settled herself upon my cock and sat bolt upright, arching her back, and displaying her firm young breasts that jutted proudly forward. Then, putting both hands behind her neck, she shook her head and looked down on me with an amused smile of sensual triumph. I thrust my hips up and down, harder and faster and my chest was soon heaving wildly with the sheer physical effort of this exciting fuck.

'Y-e-s! Y-e-s! Y-e-s!' she cried out through clenched teeth, as I met her downward pistoning with such fierce upward thrusts that soon she was clinging to me like a bareback rider on a bucking bronco in a Wild West show.

'Here I come!' I groaned as, with a huge final wrench upwards, I sent a tremendous spurt of spunk inside her seething slit. My prick tingled deliciously as I expelled jet after jet of sticky jism, and Becky's voracious cunt milked my cock until the sweet sensations of my spend died away.

The sight of this glorious fuck had stimulated Dora, who was obviously keen on being poked again by my cousin. She was on her knees with her hand around Beresford's flaccid shaft, trying with little success to coax his cock up to a further stand by licking the sensitive underside, until he said sadly, 'I'm sorry, Dora, it's no use – I've already spent four times since we came up here with Sir Loring, and my old tadger won't be in any fit state to fuck for at least another hour.'

'Are you still feeling randy, sweetie?' enquired Becky sympathetically, scrambling to her feet.

'I'm afraid that Rupert's prick is also in need of rest, but let's show the boys that we girls can enjoy ourselves even when there are no nice thick stiffies to play with.'

Dora's pretty face brightened as Becky walked across to her and, taking the eager girl by the hand, she instructed her sister (actually her half-sister, as Beresford was later to inform me) to lie down on the bed next to the still sleeping Sir Loring Sayers.

'Won't he be annoyed if we wake him up?' asked Dora.

Beresford let out a gruff laugh. 'Not really. The randy old goat will only be upset that we didn't wake him earlier!'

This answer made Dora giggle, and without further ado she parted her thighs. Becky climbed on to the bed between her sister's legs, settling herself down upon her hands and knees, and then after passing the tip of her tongue over her lips, she lowered her tousled mop of red hair and immediately began to tongue the insides of Dora's slender thighs in slow, unhurried licks, lifting her head for a moment to comment, 'Mmm, what a thick thatch of pussey hair you have, darling, but I'll have to brush it aside because it's hiding your lovely quim and that will never do. Ah, that's much better, now I can see those luscious love lips,' she added as she nuzzled her face against Dora's curly muff. 'Oh, and what a heavenly cuntal odour! I shall kiss and suck your sweet pussey and pay homage to this mossy shrine!'

I moved forward to watch Becky's pink tongue slide up and down the length of Dora's pouting love lips, before Dora moaned in ecstasy and threw her legs around her sister's neck, as Becky lapped the love juice which was pouring from Dora's cunney.

'Oooh, Becky, you are the best cunney sucker in the whole wide world!' cried Dora. 'You're making me wild with desire! Can you feel my love juice squirting all over your face?'

The lovely girl screamed out with delight as Becky slipped a hand under her bottom and started to frig her arse whilst still licking and lapping at her dripping cunney. I moved over to look at this lewd scene with rapturous attention as the girls moved themselves into a voluptuous *soixante-neuf*, licking and lapping each other's juicy quims. Despite my previous recent exertions, my shaft began to thicken as I watched Becky's juices dribble like honey from her parted pussey lips as Dora flicked her wet, darting tongue along her sister's pouting love lips.

Craning my head, I saw Becky repay the compliment by giving Dora's furry bush a thorough tonguing, soaking her curly hairs with saliva whilst she worked her tongue deeper and deeper into her sopping snatch. Becky lifted her face for a moment, and then her hand flashed out to grab my erect shaft, which by now was as hard as a bar of iron and, rubbing her hand up and down my throbbing tool, she cried out, 'Dora, you'll enjoying seeing this – watch me toss off Rupert's big stiff cock! He's going to empty his balls any second now, I can feel it! But I'm afraid you'll have to finish yourself off, Mr Mountjoy, I have to finish creaming Dora's cunney!'

She let go of my aching member and I needed no further urging to take over where she had left off. I slicked my clenched palm along my shaft, covering and uncovering my gleaming ruby knob whilst the girls' bodies jerked together in a mad erotic frenzy, and then they moaned with joy as they shuddered into a glorious mutual spend. At the same time, I drew in and held a long breath, not expelling the air until a delicious climax swept through my body and an arc of frothy spunk spurted out of my cock all over Becky's face. She yelped in delight, rubbing the sticky seed into her cheeks, and when the masculine essence had finally ceased to flow, she milked my cock of the final drains of jism by sucking out the last few drops.

In the meantime, not to be outdone, Beresford had now come over and was presenting Dora with his gigantic boner. With a squeal of delight, she gobbled his mushroomed helmet into her mouth and sucked hard on his pulsating prick, until with a little cry she released his cock from between her lips so as to point his shaft downwards to drench her titties with the jets of jism that squirted out of Beresford's throbbing tool.

As she fell back upon the pillow, at long last Sir Loring Sayers started to stir. Then his jaws fell open and he spluttered, 'Gad! What the deuce has been going on here? What have you two fillies

45

been up to whilst I was having a nap?'

'Well, we haven't been playing tiddlywinks!' answered Dora pertly.

'Now then, Dora, don't be so impertinent. I've spent enough on you to buy a new sailing dinghy!' growled the crusty baronet, to which Becky wittily retorted, 'Yes, and you've spent enough in her to launch it!'

Sir Loring joined in the general laughter, then wagged a reproving finger and exclaimed, 'You cheeky girls! You both deserve to feel the palm of my hand against your bottoms!'

'Oooh, is that a promise?' said Becky with an impudent pout.

Sir Loring seized her hand and pulled her towards him, clearing his throat and announcing, 'You've been a cheeky girl, Becky and you know what happens to cheeky girls, don't you?'

In one quick movement, he sat up and pulled the lovely girl across him, so that her superbly rounded backside was nicely exhibited to his gaze. He passed his hand lovingly over the soft satin skin of the swelling hemispheres of Becky's luscious bum, then raised his right hand and began to smack her beautiful bottom, lightly but quickly.

'Oooh! Oooh! I'm really sorry, Sir Loring, I won't be naughty again,' Becky cried out. 'Ow! Ow! Ow! Ow! That's enough! No more, I beg you! Finish me off instead with a fuck.' And she winced visibly as the colour of her bum changed from a milky white to a rosy shade of pink.

'All in good time,' snapped Sir Loring, whilst he

continued the punishment by striking alternately the left and then the right cheeks of her quivering arse. 'You richly deserve this and, besides, I adore watching your gorgeous bum and the way your cheeks jiggle when I slap them!'

In the end, however, he soon relented when Becky told him in some detail exactly how much she wanted his stiff cock inside her juicy cunt. She wriggled free and pulled off the bedclothes and clasped her fingers around his straining stiff shaft.

'Ahhh, that's better, I've had this boner since I started smacking you,' said Sir Loring with a sigh of relief.

'Have you now? Well, that's quite a cock you have there,' remarked Becky with sincere admiration, as she pulled both her hands up and down his extremely thick penis, capping and uncapping the reddish domed knob.

'It's won three Victor Pudendum [*live sex shows which were a speciality of the Jim Jam Club, which King Edward VII often attended with Lillie Langtry or the Countess of Warwick in his roisterous younger days, when he was Prince of Wales – Editor*] competitions,' said Sir Loring proudly. 'There's a full nine and a half inches in your hands, m'dear,' he added as Becky leaned forward to plant a moist kiss on his smooth wide helmet, saying, 'Would you like me to honour His Hugeness with a nice big suck?'

Sir Loring grunted his approval and lay back to enjoy himself, and Becky opened her lips and slid them over his bared bell-end. She sucked lustily on Sir Loring's knob with her tongue, and then eased her face forward to take more of the shaft inside her mouth, whilst she circled the base of his cock with one hand, working the warm velvety skin up and down, bobbing her head faster and faster in a frenetic rhythm as she gobbled on his engorged fleshy pole.

'You'd better stop, m'dear, or I'll come too quickly,' warned the baronet, and so Becky lifted her head and snuggled down next to him. In an inkling, they were entwined together and, at Sir Loring's request, I passed him one of the pillows which lay on the floor, and he inserted it under Becky's back, so that her thighs and cunney were positioned at a comfortable angle for the imminent arrival of his pulsating prick. With a surprising nimbleness for a man in his middle years, he moved himself over between Becky's legs and, nudging her knees a little further apart, he took his love truncheon in one hand and carefully guided the crown between her yielding cunney lips.

'Now is that enough cock for you?' Sir Loring politely enquired as he inserted three or four inches inside her love channel.

'No, no, I want it all,' gasped Becky, and so he drove forward, sliding his massive shaft in up to the hilt, and when it was fully ensconced inside her juicy cunt, he began to fuck the trembling girl at a slow, steady pace, pistoning his prick to and fro whilst he kissed her and cupped her ample breasts in his hands, gently pinching her erect, rubbery nipples between his thumb and fingers.

'Ah, Becky, your pussey is so delicious, so

warm and tight, and I love the way it clings round my cock,' he groaned loudly. 'Is it as good for you as it is for me?'

'Yes, yes, but let your knob stay still just a moment – it's tickling my clitty so nicely in that position,' replied Becky, closing her eyes and savouring the sensation as she slowly exhaled a deep breath. 'Aaah, that is so nice! Now fuck the arse of me, you randy old chap!'

I must say that Sir Loring was far from being pusillanimous in his fucking, and his cock sluiced in and out of Becky's cunt at an ever-increasing pace, causing her the most divine raptures, until he reached his climax and spilled his spunk into her saturated cunt whilst she twisted and bucked as she also achieved an explosive spend which, judging from the wonderful beaming smile on her face, must have sent out delicious ripples of pleasure to every fibre of her being.

Sir Loring rolled off the lovely girl and lay on his back, gasping for air, his chest heaving up and down with exhaustion. When he had caught his breath, he wiped a bead of perspiration from his brow and said admiringly, 'Damn me, Becky, but you score ten out of ten when it comes to fucking.'

'You're not so bad yourself, you old rascal,' Becky replied, giving his now limp penis a loving little squeeze. 'If I weren't a working girl, I would fuck you for free any day.'

'Thank you, m'dear, it's always most gratifying to be complimented upon one's prowess between the sheets,' said Sir Loring, hauling himself out of bed and making his way to the bathroom. 'Now I seem to recall,' he called, 'I promised to take you to that new department store in Oxford Street, to replace that pretty wrist-watch that was stolen from your apartment last week. I'll just have a wash and brush up and then, if you would like to get dressed, we'll trot along and see if we can find a suitable replacement time-piece for you.'

I raised my eyebrows when I heard this remark and uncharitably it crossed my mind that Sir Loring was foolish to believe this girl from the *demi-monde*, who had surely made up the story in order to obtain a handsome new watch. However, I was shamed when Becky raised her voice and replied, 'Thank you, Loring, that's very kind of you, but it was only an inexpensive watch that I lost and you're not to spend a lot of money, buying me a new one.' She turned to me and said, 'I wouldn't want either of you to think that I am a gold-digger, only out for what I can get from my gentlemen friends. Sir Loring wants me to have a diamond watch bracelet with a safety chain and a Russian leather case, costing twenty-five pounds, but I shan't let him buy it. I've seen a very attractive eighteen-carat gold Swiss keyless lever wrist-watch with a fifteen-carat gold bracelet in Selfridge's window. It only costs twelve pounds ten shillings and sixpence, and would make an ideal replacement.'

'And Loring has taken care of all this afternoon's expenses,' Dora advised us as she slipped on her knickers. 'Even though I know he is very wealthy, he is nonetheless a very generous man – which I find surprising because, in my experience, the richer the man, the meaner he is!'

'Time to go, old boy. I have an appointment with my tailor, and then I'm off home for a rest,' said Beresford to me, whilst we put on our clothes. 'Rupert, I'll see you tonight at Fred Nolan's apartment in Carpenter Street. I understand that the famed Mrs Beaconsfield [*one of Society's most admired cooks – Editor*] has taken over the kitchen, so we should have a damned good dinner!'

We waited for Sir Loring to return from the bathroom, then heartily thanked him and the girls for their hospitality. Before we left, I said to Dora, 'Are you going to Selfridge's with Becky? If not, you are very welcome to join me for a drink downstairs in the bar.'

'Thank you, Rupert, that would be very pleasant. Though, if it's all the same to you, I'd prefer a nice cup of tea,' she replied, and so we said goodbye to the others and sat ourselves down on a sofa by the window in one of the luxuriously furnished lounges on the first floor, overlooking the hustle and bustle of Great Windmill Street.

I ordered a pot of tea for two and a plate of assorted sandwiches, along with a small Madeira cake. For, as my old mentor Professor Webb at Oxford University was fond of saying, the worship of Venus and Priapus is tough work which requires nourishing replenishment as soon as possible afterwards.

Whilst we waited, I picked up a copy of the

Evening News and scanned the front page, snorting with irritation when I read that some foolish clerical gentleman had objected to the new carvings of Mr Epstein on the façade of the British Medical Association headquarters in the Strand because one figure, which represented Maternity, 'displayed an unseemly fecund swell'. The outraged vicar commented that 'this is a form of statuary which no careful father would wish his daughter, or no discriminating young man, his fiancée, to see.'

'I can never understand why we appear to have more than our fair share of narrow-minded people in England, whose chief pleasure in life is to keep a critical watch upon the sexual proprieties of their fellow citizens,' I commented.

Dora shrugged her shoulders and said, 'Don't attack these folk too much, Rupert. I'm sure that Madame Rosalie would tell you that they make up a large proportion of our clientele. Present company excepted, we find our services are required by the needy, not the greedy,' she added with a roguish twinkle in her eye, and smiled graciously at the portly figure of Archibald Brock-Copley, the Conservative MP for West Monmouthshire, who blew her a quick kiss as he strode out of the lounge into the hall.

'And you must surely except old Archie. I've heard it said that he will poke any female between the ages of sixteen and sixty.' Grinning, I related to Dora the true story of how, on one wild night last year at the Jim Jam, the lusty politician had fucked one of the Club's cooks, two housemaids and Miss Gertrude Wiggins, the popular *ingenue* now appearing in Mr Shaw's new play *Man and Superman* at the Royal Court Theatre.

'Ah, well, one must allow the poor chap a certain latitude,' remarked Dora, as a waitress appeared and set down our tea on the table in front of us. 'Why, at home he is allowed his conjugal rights only twice a month at best. And I am reliably informed that, even then, his wife has been known to read the newspaper whilst Archie is heaving away. So it is little wonder that he looks elsewhere to satisfy his needs – which is good news as far as I am concerned – he is a most generous gentleman,' she added as she poured out two cups of tea. 'Milk and sugar, Rupert?'

'Yes, please,' I said, but then a frown formed across my brow as I remembered a recent heated discussion Beresford and myself had had with Archie. He had attempted to pooh-pooh the need to improve the lot of the working classes, but we supported the need to alleviate the distressing conditions in the slums which disfigure almost all our major cities.

'The ordinary man in the street is perfectly contented to go without things he has never used,' he had argued when Beresford put forward the case for giving special help to the thousands of unemployed and casual labourers in the East End of London. 'And the working classes only become dissatisfied with their lot when they are egged on to cause trouble by greedy Socialist and Anarchist agitators. Fortunately, the vast majority of our citizens are happy to let their favoured superiors govern them.

'Mind, I do agree that some way should be found of helping the deserving poor, who have been brought to misfortune through no fault of their own. But we must always be careful to relieve their distress in a manner which will not give any encouragement to idleness and vice.'

I relayed his words to Dora now, and she nodded her head. 'It's very strange how, in general terms, Archie can speak about his fearful concern that, by helping people in need, he might demoralise them, whilst in his private life he allows the natural kindness of his heart to overrule the cold economic dictates of his head.'

'Indeed, and do you speak about Archie from any personal experience?' I asked.

She hesitated for a moment, before replying.

'Yes, I do. But you are probably aware that for all the girls living at Madame Rosalie's, it is one of the strictest rules of the house that we must never gossip about any of the gentlemen or ladies who visit us.'

I filed a note in my memory to question Dora further about whether she had any female clients, for I have always enjoyed hearing of an uninhibited tribadic tale. [*In the eighteenth and nineteenth centuries, lesbians were known as 'tribades'. The word derives from the Latin word 'tribus', to rub – Editor*]. However, this could wait until a later time, and so I said, 'Well, you are hardly giving away any secret information about Archie. It's an open secret that he uses the facilities of your house so often that Madame Rosalie charges him specially discounted rates!'

This made Dora chuckle, and she picked up her handbag and rummaged inside it until she found an envelope. Holding it in her hand, she said, 'Rupert, please give me your word of honour that you will not disclose a word of this letter from Archie to anyone else, not even Beresford, without first obtaining my permission.'

'You have my word,' I said instantly, and reached out for the letter. Surprisingly, Archie had written to Dora on House of Commons notepaper, which itself was surely taking an unnecessary risk. Be that as it may, his *billet-doux* read as follows:

My Darling Dora,

After leaving you late last night, I took a taxi-cab back to my rooms in The Adelphi, but I could hardly sleep a wink, for my cock kept rising up and demanding to be buried once again inside your juicy cunt! And when at last I finally managed to doze off for forty winks, I dreamed that I was back in bed with you at Madame Rosalie's, with your gorgeous bottom perched over my face so that I could kiss and suck your lovely pussey!

Since then, I have been thinking about your Uncle Joseph, whom you told me was so badly injured by a motor vehicle last month. As the poor old chap cannot give the police any details of the car involved, it seems most doubtful that we will ever discover the identity of the villain who knocked him off his bicycle and then drove off without seeing if he could offer any assistance.

I shall raise the matter of these 'hit and run'

motorists with the Home Secretary, and ask for a more
stringent punishment to be set for those found guilty of
the offence. But this will be of little comfort to your
uncle, who will lose at least eight weeks' wages whilst
he recovers from his broken ankle. At least he is
fortunate enough to work for a good employer who has
promised to offer him another job when he is able to
return to work, although it will not be so well-paid as
his previous position, which he will no longer be
physically able to perform.

Therefore, I am enclosing a postal order for twenty
pounds, which I would like you to give to your uncle. I
hope it will assist his family through this time of trial.
All I ask in return, Dora, is that you send on this
money with no mention of from whence it came, for I do
not wish to publicise any contributions I may make to
the many good causes which lay claim to my attention,
and always send my donations on an anonymous basis.

Meanwhile, give my love to your delightful cunney
which, all being well, I look forward to fucking next
Wednesday afternoon.
From your own ever devoted admirer,
Archie

'Well, well, well. So there is another, more human
side to Archie after all,' I murmured, giving back
the letter. 'Do tell me where you met him – have
you know him for long?'

'Only about six months,' she replied, offering
me another sandwich.

Not finding any of my favourite kind, I stopped
Mrs Harrison, the Club's housekeeper, who
happened to be passing by, and asked why there

were no cucumber sandwiches on the plate.

'I'm so sorry, Mr Mountjoy, there were no cucumbers at Covent Garden this morning, not even for ready money,' she replied as she swept by. 'Oh, and by the way, your account is overdue, Mr Mountjoy. Would you please give Miss O'Neill a cheque before you leave the Club this afternoon?'

Dora chuckled. 'That will teach you to complain! Anyhow, you asked me where I first met Archie, and the answer is at his home near Dorking in Surrey. It was on a fine August day last summer, and Becky and I had decided to put our bicycles on the train and spend a day in the country. We spent an enjoyable day, riding around Dorking and had luncheon at the King's Head in North Street.'

'Ah, that's the public house upon which Dickens is supposed to have based the Marquis of Granby in *Pickwick Papers*,' I chimed in.

'Yes,' Dora went on, 'the day turned out to have several literary associations, for we journeyed to Deepdene, where Disraeli wrote *Coningsby* and then on to Fanny Burney's house opposite Burford Bridge [*Alas, the original house was burned down in 1919 – Editor*] where she entertained Sir Walter Scott. It was there that we bumped into your old chum Frank Folkestone, who happened to be visiting Sir Raymond and Lady Fairclough, some old friends who lived nearby. It was quite a coincidence, seeing him there, for only a few weeks earlier he had met Becky at the lawn tennis championships at Wimbledon. She had been engaged as an escort for the Duke of Padua who, as you probably know, is of the homosexualist persuasion, but who could hardly take one of his young men to sit with Queen Alexandra in the Royal Box!

'Well, Frank invited us to take tea at Sir Raymond's, who he said would be delighted to welcome us, but I guessed that he would appreciate some time alone together with Becky (nor would she be averse to the idea, for a mutual acquaintance had informed us, only a day before, of the enormous girth of Frank's colossal cock) so I said to them that if Frank would be kind enough to give me the directions to Sir Raymond Fairclough's house, I would meet them there a little later, because I wanted to take some photographs of the lovely scenery with my new Brownie camera.

'So Frank informed me how to get to Fairclough Lodge, which was less than a mile away, and I left the pair to walk there by themselves, whilst I rode into a forest of box trees, disregarding the 'Private: No Trespassers' sign. Soon I found a small grassy glade where I dismounted and, leaning my bicycle against a tree, I took out the light blanket I had folded into the saddle-bag and, using the bag as a pillow, I lay down in the beautifully shaded sunlight.

'In fact, it was so hot that I decided to see for myself whether there was anything in this new fad of naturism practised by a sizeable number of people on the Continent. Amongst their beliefs, naturists hold that sunlight is highly beneficial in small doses and that we should expose even our private parts. This seemed highly unlikely to me, but the only way to find out was to test the theory for myself.

'There did not appear to be anyone nearby, and I doubted if many people would be walking through this sleepy little wood. So I quickly undressed and lay on my back. Then I turned over to lie face down, exposing my naked bum cheeks to the warm sunshine, for I had also brought with me a copy of the *Ladies Pictorial*. I spread the magazine in front of me and began to read one of Miss Barbara Boote's exciting romantic stories.

'But I had only been lying there for about ten minutes when I thought I heard the rustle of footsteps. I raised my head and looked around but there appeared to be nobody in the vicinity and I went back to reading my magazine. Then I heard the noise again and decided I was definitely being watched – but by whom? I took a small pair of field glasses from my bag and whilst pretending to be reading the magazine, which I held as close to my face as possible, I scoured the landscape around me and sure enough, I saw four gentlemen hiding behind a clump of bushes some seventy or eighty yards away. By chance, one of them moved to take up a better position, and I recognised his face from the Jim Jam Club.'

'Tut tut, was this Peeping Tom anyone I know?' I asked, thinking to myself that perhaps such a matter should be reported to the Club's disciplinary committee, of which I was a member.

A wide grin spread across her face. 'Oh yes,

although I don't think he deserves a derogatory epithet, for he had not gone for a walk in the woods with the intention of spying on courting couples, and he must have been quite shocked to come across a girl stretched out naked on a rug on the grass. Anyhow, the gentleman concerned was none other than the distinguished Member of Parliament, Mr Archibald Brock-Copley!

'Strangely enough, the idea that Archie was staring at my nude breasts and fluffy thatch of pussey hair somehow both annoyed and excited me, and so I decided to put on a special erotic show for him. I began by massaging my nipples, rubbing and squeezing them against my palm until they stood up like two ripe rubbery bullets. This made me feel so horny that I started to frig myself, slipping the tip of my forefinger in and out of my crack, and I was getting really carried away, and writhing in genuine pleasure as a series of little spends crackled through my body. Soon I was so far gone that I called out, "Archie, I know you're hiding over there! Come here this instant and fuck me, you naughty boy!"

'I must admit that he was not slow to obey, and almost at once he was at my side, pulling down his trousers and drawers to bare his succulent swollen shaft. "M'mm, that meaty cock looks good enough to eat," I exclaimed, and as I sat up and cradled his hot, velvet-skinned chopper in my hands, my hair tumbled over my face. Then I looked up to see his excited flushed face and the well-endowed Member for West Monmouthshire and I exchanged a broad smile before I moistened my lips and slid them over his thick prick, which glided smoothly into my mouth and down my throat.

'Archie fucked my mouth with style, pumping his fat shaft between my lips faster and faster until I could feel his heavy balls slapping against my chin. My own climax was building quickly, then I felt his fingers running through my hair and suddenly he grunted, his body went rigid, and then his cock spurted out jet after jet of salty spunk into my mouth.

' "A-a-r-g-h!" he gurgled with delight as I gulped it all down, swallowing every drop of his copious emission until he withdrew his tool from my mouth and I lay back on the blanket, gasping for air.

' "Now it's my turn to bring you off," he panted and slid himself down between my legs and buried his face between my thighs, wiggling his tongue all around my juicy crack. My senses reeled and I moaned out loudly as the tip of Archie's tongue flicked against my clitty, sending tingling pulses of pleasure shooting through me. I pulled his face tightly against my pussey. His lips pressed against my curly thatch and his tongue prodded through my pouting lips, which really drove me wild with desire.

' "Archie, I'm ready for you," I gasped, taking hold of his broad shoulders and pulling him up over my trembling body.

' "And I'm ready for you, Dora," he replied with a wolfish grin, and then he kissed me, exploring the deepest recesses of my mouth with his eager tongue whilst I spread my legs as wide as possible, keeping my hand on his prick to guide his knob inside my yearning wet cunt. Goodness me, how incredibly aroused I became when Archie sank his still stiff boner into my squelchy love channel, pounding into me with an almost frightening power.

'It turned out to be a very quick coupling, as we were both perhaps overexcited but, oh, how we enjoyed that passionate fuck on that warm summer day. I will never forget how, with every thrust of Archie's superb shaft, my own hips thrust back, kissing his cock with my clinging cunney muscles.

'I cried out, "My God, I'm going to spend again! Fill my cunt with spunky cream, Archie!" His wiry body went rigid, he let out a low growl, then shot a thrilling torrent of gushing seed into my cunt, before his body relaxed and he pressed his lithe frame slowly down on top of me, carefully keeping his cock inside my cunney as we calmed down.

'At last we rolled apart, absolutely exhausted by this frenetic bout of love-making, to the applause of Archie's friends, who had ventured near for a closer view. All three of them had unbuttoned their trousers, and had brought out their tools to frig themselves whilst watching us. I was especially taken by the girth of one particular prick which belonged to a Parliamentary collea-gue and close chum of Archie, Captain Robert Cripps, who represents a Kentish constituency. But although I was tempted by the Captain's thick cock, there was really no time left to take part in any more fun and games. So Archie and I dressed ourselves and the four gentlemen escorted me back to the road where we made our farewells and I cycled back to Fairclough Lodge where I joined Becky, Frank and Sir Raymond and Lady Fairclough for tea.

'Later on, whilst we waited at Dorking Station for the train back to London, Becky informed me that she and Frank had found the opportunity to enjoy a fine fuck behind the greenhouse in Sir Raymond's garden, so all in all we both had a splendid day down in the country.' Dora looked at her watch. 'My, it's almost half past four,' she said. 'I really must be going. So nice to have met you, Rupert. I do hope we'll see each other again.'

'I'm sure we will,' I said, heaving myself up from my chair as Dora rose to her feet. 'And do give my kindest regards to Becky.'

I walked with her as far as the ladies cloakroom and, after saying goodbye in the hall, decided to while away the time till six o'clock, when I would speak on the telephone to Amber, with a well-earned snooze.

CHAPTER TWO

Guess Who's Coming To Dinner

I ENJOYED A JOLLY GOOD KIP for an hour or so until, as I had instructed him, one of the Club servants gently shook my shoulder and woke me up. 'It's five minutes to six, Mr Mountjoy,' he informed me. After thanking him, I went down to the telephone office to see if they were able to connect me with Lady Amber Berlynne up in Chester. Happily, there were no difficulties, and I was able to speak briefly to the lovely Amber. She was thrilled when I told her that I would be delighted to travel up North on Friday week, to join her party and watch the Grand National steeplechase.

'You'll receive my telegram later this evening,' I said, and Amber replied excitedly, 'That's wonderful, Rupert, I'm so looking forward to seeing you again. Now, I have some good news for you – I guessed you would come if you possibly could, so I asked the Adelphi Hotel to let me know if a room became available for the Grand National weekend. Well, they called me less than an hour ago to say that there had been a cancellation, so I have booked the room in your name for the Friday and Saturday nights.'

'Excellent! Now I won't have to worry about finding a place to rest my weary head,' I remarked, and she giggled and said, 'Well, there should never have been any doubt on that score, Rupert. Surely, you knew full well that you would be sleeping with your face tucked between my thighs, because you know how I adore the way you lick out my cunney!'

With a disapproving cluck, I rebuked her, trying to keep my voice severe: 'Shush, you bad girl, or I'll smack your bottom when I get up to Liverpool.'

'Oooh, do you promise?' she asked sweetly. 'Darling, I think this is Mama coming down the stairs. Write to me soon, but in the meantime, I'll tell Mr Foxall Keene you'll be joining the party, and I look forward to seeing you on Friday week at the Adelphi Hotel.'

'You will indeed,' I agreed, blowing her a kiss down the telephone. 'Goodbye for now, Amber. I'll write to you before I leave London.'

I put down the telephone and sauntered down to the writing room, where I dashed off a brief note to Goldhill, our old family retainer at Albion Towers, my parents' home in Yorkshire, asking him which horse I should back in the big race. Over the years, Goldhill has provided me with some first-class tips, being an avid follower of the sport of kings and (even more important) having the great advantage of inside information pro-vided by a nephew who was employed as a head lad in one of the large training stables in Lambourn.

Then the porter called a taxi to drive me back to Bedford Square, for I wanted to shower and shave before setting off for my dinner engagement at Frederick Nolan's luxurious Mayfair rooms. As I put on my dinner suit, which Edwards had laid across my bed, I allowed myself a chuckle, recalling my part in acting as a cameraman in the American cinematographer's *tableau vivant* film shot in the forest near Knaresborough. [*See* An Edwardian Dandy I: Youthful Scandals *for full details. Unfortunately, no copies of this early sex film have survived – a great pity, although it was not the first European blue movie to be made. This honour probably goes to* Le Tub, *a short three-minute film made by the French pioneer Georges Meliès, using the then newly-developed Lumière brothers' equipment – Editor*] A mutual friend of Mr Nolan and myself, the theatrical impresario Mr Charles Viney, had kindly called me the previous day, offering me transport to and from the dinner, and on the dot of half past seven, I saw his new Austin York Landaulette pull up outside the house.

'Good night, Edwards. I shall probably be back around midnight,' I said to my footman, as he helped me on with my overcoat and passed me my silk hat.

'Good night, sir, I hope you enjoy a pleasant evening,' he answered, and then added hesitantly as he opened the front door, 'If there is any chance of obtaining Miss Macnamara's autograph, sir, I would be very much obliged.'

'I'll do what I can,' I promised, and strode out towards the big forty-horse-power car. 'Hello, Charles. Thank you again for calling for me,' I said, climbing into the passenger compartment and plumping myself down next to him. 'What a splendid new car!'

'My pleasure, Rupert. You're hardly taking me out of my way,' he replied genially. 'I'm looking forward to this evening. One always dines well with Hetty Beaconsfield in the kitchen, and I wouldn't be surprised if Fred has a surprise or two up his sleeve for Maisie Macnamara. He wants her to appear in one of his films, even though the audience won't be able to hear her sing! I suppose he believes that her name will bring in the customers, but I still feel that this bioscope [*an early term for the cinema, though still in use in South Africa until quite recently – Editor*] is a nine-day wonder. Mark my words, it will never replace live theatre.'

I said, 'Well, you know your own business, of course, but what will happen if some clever Johnny invents a process to marry sound to film?'

'I'll worry about that when it happens,' declared Charles. Then he poked me in the ribs with his elbow and gave a fat chuckle, and added, 'On the other hand, I wish I could show Fred's latest little masterpiece at the Holborn Empire. If what I hear about the film is true, even at ten shillings [*50p – Editor*] there would be queues running all the way down to Gray's Inn Road!'

Jackson, Charles's chauffeur, skilfully manoeuvred us through the heavy West End traffic, asking and giving no quarter, as is the way in London these days. As we were crossing Oxford Circus, forced to brake sharply by a taxi-cab cutting across us, he shouted a fulsome imprecation at the errant driver, before turning round to apologise to us for the jerky ride.

'Sorry about the sudden stop, gentlemen, but some of those bloody cabbies want horse-whipping, the way they cut in and out without a thought for anyone else, the bastards.'

'Yes, it must be most annoying,' said Charles soothingly. 'But we are in no great hurry and I suppose that the cab drivers are always under pressure to get to their destination as quickly as possible. After all, most people who hail a taxi are in a hurry and urge the driver to get to wherever they want to go at top speed – I know I do!'

We were now held up in a mêlée of cars, taxis and buses in Oxford Street. Charles winked at me, then leaned forward to tap Jackson on the shoulder and said, 'In any case, Jackson, you shouldn't be bothered by a bit of traffic after our little tryst with Tessa Hardwick this afternoon. Oh, don't worry,' he continued as the chauffeur turned round with an embarrassed expression of surprise on his face. 'We don't have to mince words in front of Mr Mountjoy.'

Charles turned to me and added, 'Tessa is a young soubrette who came along to my offices in Shaftesbury Avenue, to a preliminary audition for a new musical play I am staging at the Alhambra in June. She's an attractive girl with a fine, full figure and the most voluptuously rounded breasts that you could wish to see. Of course, when she came to my office I could only see the outline of her bosoms against her tight creamy silk blouse. As fate would have it, five minutes after she arrived I received a telephone call from Charing Cross Hospital to say that Professor Godfrey, the pianist whom she had engaged to accompany her, had been knocked down by a bus in Trafalgar Square and was being treated for concussion.

'Tessa's face fell, but I told her that if she gave me her music I should be able to take his place. She brightened up when she heard this and said, "Oh, you are kind, Mr Viney. I thought I would sing 'Burlington Bertie' and 'Just Like the Ivy', and then a song which Professor Godfrey and I composed together last week."

' "You only have to give me the music for your own song," I said as I sat down at the piano. "As for the others, I could play those with a blindfold round my eyes. Just tell me in which key you want to sing."

'I thought at the time that she gave me an odd little look, but we began with those two favourite music-hall numbers, which she warbled rather well. Then she passed me the music for her own song, 'A Maiden's Wish', saying, "The professor hasn't written down the words on the sheet, but that presents no problem because I know them by heart." I ran through the simple melody and after Tessa had told me at what speed she wished the ballad to be played, I introduced the song with a rousing flourish. But only seconds later, it was all

I could do to stop myself falling off the piano stool as I listened to her sing the first verse:

"When wishes first enter a young maiden's breast,
She longs by her lover to be firmly caressed;
She longs with her lover to do the old trick,
As in truth what she wants is a taste of his prick!
Her cunney is itching from morn until night
And only his prick can yield her delight;
She would like very well to be laid on the grass,
And have two ample bollocks slapping up 'gainst
    her arse."

' "Good grief, you can't sing that in a public theatre!" I spluttered as Tessa drew breath to begin the chorus. She looked at me with a quizzical expression, and said coolly, "Of course I couldn't, but if you ever get called to put on one of those special smoking-room shows at a country house party, that song would go down well, wouldn't it?"

' "I dare say it would," I agreed. Then she said to me with a twinkle in her eye: "Mr Viney, all this singing makes me very thirsty. Could I possibly trouble you for something to drink?"

' "Of course you may, Tessa," I said, and walked over to the bookcase, pulling it to one side to reveal my new Ice Cabinette. "Would a glass of champagne be acceptable?"

' "Champagne is always acceptable," she replied in her sibilant, sultry voice, "especially when it comes from a new friend. Tell me though, can I celebrate getting a part in the new show?"

' "Tessa, I really can't give you any cast-iron guarantees," I replied cautiously. "But I can certainly say that you have passed the first stage. Now I cannot speak for the director, who has the final say on casting, and I don't want to give you any 'smooth comforts false' as the Bard puts it, but I think I can safely say that, at the very least, we should be able to offer you a minor role." '

Now, along with many other fellow members of the Jim Jam Club, I had always joshed Charles Viney about the magnificent leather Chesterfield sofa in his office, saying that no chorus girl ever managed to get on stage without first being fucked by Charles on this 'casting couch', as cousin Beresford calls it – and at this point I took the opportunity of reminding Charles how he had always hotly denied this charge.

He had the grace to throw up his hands in surrender and admit: 'Well, I still maintain that female artistes get to the top through their talent, but I dare say that, in my experience, the sucking of an important prick never did an ambitious girl any harm.'

'And of course the fact that Tessa Hardwick gained a part in the new musical comedy at the Alhambra had nothing to do with the fact that she gobbled your chopper,' I said sarcastically – and somewhat crudely – as I tried to keep a note of envy from creeping into my voice.

Charles gave a wicked grin. 'Rupert, how can you jump to such a cynical conclusion? Tessa has a lovely voice and a powerful stage presence and I would have cast her as Minnie Smith, the pretty village girl being wooed by the squire's son, even if she had been totally unfriendly at the audition.'

'Pull the other one, old boy,' I grunted, but Charles shook his head vigorously. 'Not guilty, your honour, though it's true that Tessa became *very* friendly after the audition, and when we happened to find ourselves sitting on my Chesterfield, uh, my hands seemed to be drawn like magnets to her large bosoms when we exchanged a friendly kiss.

' "Would you like to see my breasts in all their glory?" she enquired, letting her hand fall on the bulge in my lap, and then she giggled and went on: "Oh, yes, the state of your prick answers my question. Poor cocky! It must be so uncomfortable, having to stand so stiffly in such a cramped space. Let me relieve this dreadful confinement."

'To my delight, she unbuttoned my flies and fished out my throbbing shaft. Our mouths met in a lingering passionate kiss, whilst I helped her to wriggle out of her clothes. We only broke off the kiss when she pulled her chemise over her head, and then she swiftly rolled down her knickers and I drank in the awesome beauty of her gorgeous naked body.

'Believe me, Rupert, I have seen many bosoms in my time, but the exciting swell of her bare young breasts were perhaps the most perfect I have ever seen, firm and globular, each looking a little way from each other, and both topped with rich crimson nipples which were as hard as rocks – I massaged them somewhat shyly, for I could scarcely believe my good fortune.

'Meanwhile she stroked my cock with her long fingers and lay back on the sofa, holding my shaft in her hand and pressing it against her belly before pulling it forwards into the valley between her delicious soft globes, and I rubbed my prick against her taut titties whilst she cupped my balls in her hands. Then I moved my cock up further and brought my helmet to her waiting lips and Tessa took my tool inside her wet, willing mouth and gave me a most wonderful sucking-off.

'Then, just before I was about to spend, the wanton girl rolled me over on my back and climbed up over my quivering, stiff cock. I slipped my hands around those luscious breasts whilst she lowered herself down on my bursting boner, but she had only time to begin bouncing up and down on my shaft when there was a knock, and the door opened and this fellow,' – and here Charles pointed at the chauffeur, who suddenly began to make a close study of the advertisement on the back of the stationary omnibus in front of us – 'walked in. But instead of being enraged by this intrusion, Tessa squealed, ''Terence Jackson! Fancy seeing you here! Why, I haven't seen you since you were driving for the Bishop of Middlesex.''

' ''You know each other?'' I said weakly, and Tessa nodded and explained that she and my chauffeur had grown up together in a small village on the outskirts of Northampton. ''Mind you, the town would have been better called Littlehampton as far as the girls were concerned – there were so few sturdy thick pricks around for us to play with," panted Tessa as she continued to ride her oily cunney up and down my trembling cock. "But Terry was the exception to the rule – he must have had the biggest prick in the county dangling between his legs. Oooh, I wonder if you would mind if he joined us and fucked my botty – I noticed you had some butter in the ice-box, and he could smear some on his shaft." '

I could see the back of Jackson's neck redden as he engaged first gear and we crawled forward a few yards. 'She was certainly a cool little miss and no mistake,' I commented.

'I'll say she was, though Jackson here needed no second invitation. "How are you, Tessa? I saw you at the Finsbury Park Empire a few months ago," he gabbled, tearing off his clothes. "You should have come backstage afterwards, I'd have been glad to see you," she rejoined, to which I rather wittily said, "Well, now he has an even better chance to look up an old friend!" And this remark made Tessa scream with laughter. As she requested, Jackson greased his sizeable weapon with some butter and once he had positioned himself behind her, he found little difficulty in inserting his knob between the plump cheeks of her backside.

'Jackson's helmet was soon well burrowed in Tessa's bottom and, clamping his knees on either side of her waist, he held her firmly until his shaft was fully sheathed inside her. At first Tessa experienced some slight discomfort, but then she groaned with delight and wiggled her bum to each sawing motion of Jackson's prick, and I too jerked my hips up and down in time with his rhythm. We could feel our two cocks throbbing against each other, separated only by the thin membrane of the anal canal, and both of us spent very quickly. I came first, injecting the gorgeous girl with jets of bubbling spunk, and moments later Jackson discharged a gush of jism into Tessa's bottom. Then he slowly withdrew his shaft with a faint "pop" and sank down beside us.'

As if by magic, the traffic cleared in front of us and just five minutes later, Jackson was pulling up outside Fred Nolan's apartment in an opulent mansion block in Carpenter Street. As he stepped out smartly to open the passenger door for us, Charles said, 'Jackson, you may leave the car for a short time to answer any calls of nature. I believe the tradesmen's entrance is round the corner over on the left. You will also obtain some tasty refreshment in Mr Nolan's kitchen, as he has hired a noted cook for the evening.'

'Who might that be, sir? Surely not Mrs Beaconsfield?'

'Right in one, Jackson,' I answered, while Charles rang the doorbell. 'With any luck, she will have baked a selection of her famous cakes, so we shall all be in for a treat.'

The door opened and, to my surprise, the hired manservant (for Fred Nolan only stayed in his London home for short periods of time; he often rented it out during the Season, and when he did take up residence, rather than take on permanent domestics, he hired the necessary staff from Aspiso's agency in Clerkenwell) who was acting as butler for the evening was none other than Lawbress, my former footman.

'Good evening, sir! How pleasant to see you again – I trust you are keeping well,' said Lawbress as I passed him my hat and coat.

'I'm very well, thank you, Lawbress,' I replied. 'But what are you doing here? I thought you were in service with Sir Rodney and Lady Brampton down in Sussex.'

'So I was, sir, along with Mary,' he answered, referring to the housemaid who had left my employ at the same time as Lawbress. He folded Charles Viney's evening cape and hat over his arm. 'But Sir Rodney closed the house last November when he sailed with his family to Buenos Aires, to take up his appointment as the British Ambassador to Argentina. So Mary and I set up house together in a little flat off the Fulham Road. Aspiso's keep us busy enough with temporary work such as tonight, especially since we can be relied upon to be discreet. Also, we're in great demand to perform special services at bachelor parties,' he added mysteriously. Then our host came out from the drawing-room to greet us in person.

'Charles, Rupert! So glad you could come at such short notice,' he welcomed us. 'Come inside and meet some of the other guests. Ah, but first let me give you your badges,' he continued, giving us both bright blue buttons with the letters 'K.O.M.' spelled out on them. 'I'd be obliged if you would pin these on your jackets.'

'By all means, Fred,' I said, scratching my head. 'But what on earth is the purpose behind them? Are you forming a new political party?'

The elegant American clapped me on the shoulder. 'I suppose I am, in a manner of speaking,' he chuckled, and threw open the door of the drawing-room. 'The badges signify founder membership of a most exclusive group – the "Keen On Macnamara" society.' [*The first fan clubs for show-business personalities sprang up around the turn of the century – one of the earliest centred around the matinée idol Lewis Waller – and the Edwardians were great autograph collectors – Editor*].

'Now, I need hardly introduce you to your cousin Beresford,' continued Fred as he ushered us in. 'But I don't think either you or Charles have had the pleasure of meeting two budding thespians, Miss Norma Wharton and Miss Suzie Wingate, the leading ladies in my latest film.'

I looked across the sumptuously furnished room to where two pretty young wenches were sitting together on a settee. Norma was the elder of the two, in her early twenties and of a slender build, with shoulder-length reddish-brown hair which seemed to shine in the glow of the bright electric light from the lampstand beside her. Suzie, who could not have been more than nineteen at most, sported a mane of silky blonde hair and was blessed with a most beautiful complexion, large blue eyes, a cheeky *retroussé* nose and an impish smile.

Fred completed the introductions, and as I

shook hands with the two girls I commented that, delighted as I was to make their acquaintance, I was rather surprised that they were such ardent devotees of Maisie Macnamara.

'Well, to be quite honest, we're not as enthusiastic about her as Fred,' confessed Suzie, as I picked up a glass of champagne from the silver tray which Lawbress proffered. 'I mean, we do admire her, but I would prefer to join a "K.O.C." society.'

' "K.O.C."? Let me think a moment,' I said, furrowing my brow as I considered to whom Suzie might be attracted. 'H'mm, could that be "Keen On Clifford", by any chance?'

'Oh, you *are* clever, Mr Mountjoy!' How did you guess?' exclaimed the pretty girl, but I refused to accept any great praise, and with a modest smile, replied, 'Well, it was hardly a difficult problem to solve. Martin Harvey and Arthur Clifford are the two actors whom most women swoon over these days and as I had the clue of an initial, it was easy to work out the answer. But our host just announced that you and Miss Wharton have leading roles in his latest film, so may I presume that you both appeared on the stage? You must both forgive me, but I don't believe that I have seen either of you perform.'

'You wouldn't have done unless you lived in East Anglia,' said Suzie with a sweet smile. 'And then, the only theatrical experience Norma and I have had was with Mr Brindsley Hopcraft's repertory company, which tours the small theatres of Norfolk and Suffolk.'

I looked around for Charles, and saw him in a huddle with Fred and Beresford in the far corner of the room. 'Ah, in that case,' I said, sipping my champagne, 'you must have words later with Charles Viney over there. He is an impresario, you know, and owns three music hall theatres in the provinces, besides having three plays currently running in the West End.'

'Yes, but unfortunately we have never actually acted, as such,' Norma said wryly. 'I was in charge of the company's wardrobe and Suzie was my assistant – but occasionally we appeared on stage as maids in drawing-room comedies, or in crowd scenes when Mr Hopcraft put on a Shakespeare play.'

'That's how we came to meet Fred,' explained Suzie. 'We were playing a summer season in Ipswich, and we arrived back at our digs in a little village out of town one day, with the intention of spending a free afternoon in the fresh air. Norma and I made up a picnic before going for a walk to a local park, and we were simply strolling along when Fred came over and asked us if we would mind being in a film he was making of an English summer scene for a chain of American nickelodeons [*the early American cinemas which charged 5 cents for admission – Editor*].'

Whilst Suzie was talking I had heard the doorbell ring out and seen Fred slip out into the hall to welcome the new arrivals. Now he reappeared with none other than Lady Beth Prickett, one of the merriest young sparks in London society. A lass who loved nothing better than to wear the most daring low-cut dresses that accentuated the soft curves of her creamy white breasts and barely covered her thrusting nipples, she was also blessed with a happy disposition, and I had always been captivated by the two cheeky dimples which appeared when her full vermilion lips broke out into laughter.

The other male guests were all known to Beth, but naturally she had never met Norma and Suzie before, and although they were obviously from a social class considerably below her own, she chatted to the two girls as though to equals. She was followed five minutes later by the final guest, Megan Furzehill, the 'Society Suffragette' as the newspapers dubbed her, who had achieved national notoriety by tipping a pot of yellow paint over the Reverend Jeffrey Collins, one of the self-appointed leaders of the Anti-Suffrage faction, after he had written in the *Morning Post* that those women who were convicted of offences during suffragette demonstrations should have their hair cut off and be deported to the Colonies.

I must say, I was taken with the looks of this feisty girl. Her twinkling dark eyes and high cheekbones were set off by a mass of brown curls, and she was wearing a fetching green off-the-shoulder gown which showed that, like Beth, she had also been endowed with sizeable rounded bosoms which spilled out over the top of her low-cut *décolletage*.

Shortly afterwards, Lawbress announced that dinner was served, and together – I partnering Suzie, Beresford with Norma on his arm and

Charles escorting Megan – we trooped into the luxuriously appointed dining-room to the strains of the latest Maisie Macnamara gramophone record. Fred and Beth followed, gaily singing the chorus of:

Oh, you don't know Maisie like I do,
Said the naughty little bird on Maisie's hat!

As we took our seats, Fred tapped his wine glass with a spoon and said, 'Ladies and gentlemen, before we dine, I have an important if rather sad announcement to make. Our guest of honour, Miss Maisie Macnamara, can alas only be with us tonight in spirit. The Countess of Warwick has asked her to Easton Lodge to appear in an entertainment for her distinguished house guests, who I understand will include Tum-Tum [*Society's private* lese-majesty *nickname for the portly King Edward VII – Editor*] and Mrs Keppel, so you will understand that she could hardly refuse this unofficial royal command.'

'What a shame! Still, at least Maisie is safe from any unwanted attention from His Majesty, since he will be busy enough, satisfying the needs of Mrs Keppel and Daisy Warwick,' Charles commented drily, and Beresford chuckled, 'Absolutely! Although she will have to bolt her bedroom door if the King is being attended by Sir Barry Grey or Colonel Bob Topping – and of course her absence doesn't prevent us drinking a toast to Maisie's very good health!'

Well, suffice it to say that we drank this and

several other toasts whilst consuming the excellent dinner that Mrs Hetty Beaconsfield had prepared for us. Our host had spared no expense, and I reproduce the menu here:

Caviare

*

Tortue Claire

*

Salade de Homard

*

Riz de Veau aux Epinards

*

Poulet à le Bechamel

*

Selle d'Agneau

*

Omelette Surprise

*

Charlotte Russe – Gâteau d'abricot à la Suisse – Tarte aux Pommes

*

Fraises – Ananas – Pêches

*

Café Turc – Thé Russe

And this lavish fare was washed down by a selection of the finest wines; I was not the only gentleman to stagger slightly as we rose from our chairs when the ladies retired to the drawing-room.

Lawbress handed round a box of Cuban Corona Coronas, but I was pleased that only

Beresford lit up a cigar, for since I gave up smoking on the advice of Doctor Jonathan Letchmore, I find the smell of even the finest tobacco distasteful. I was not averse, however, to finishing the meal with a glass of Fred's '87 Sandeman port.

'I was surprised that the subject of your latest masterpiece never arose during dinner,' I remarked, filling my glass and then passing the decanter to Charles Viney. 'Even Norma and Suzie, who appeared in the film, kept somewhat quiet about it. Why, I don't even know what it's called – have you a projector in the house, so we can see it later this evening?'

Fred shrugged his shoulders and said, 'Well, I didn't want to talk about it, in case I embarrassed the girls. You see, I made a short movie of the English countryside, but I also filmed Norma and Suzie in tribadic play, which should earn a small fortune when I sail back to New York next week.'

'You lucky chap!' said Beresford enviously, puffing on his giant cigar. 'Well, at least you can tell us all about it whilst the girls are out of the room.'

'There really isn't that much to tell,' Fred replied. 'One has to be very careful when asking girls whether they would like to take part in a *risqué* film. However, I judged that Norma and Suzie were game girls, who would each be extremely happy to earn a twenty pound appearance fee. Once they agreed, I took them across into the grounds of Lord Lempert's estate (for I was a house guest of this noble peer who has a keen interest in cinematography) and into the main house, where I had set up my apparatus in an empty bedroom. The story of the film is that Suzie is surprised by an unexpected visit from her friend whilst she is changing her clothes and, well, things start to get a little wild.'

'You can say that again,' said a female voice behind me, and I whirled round to see that the four girls had trooped in from the drawing-room.

'Good heavens, what are you doing here?' gasped Beresford.

'Why should we be excluded from the table just so you men can tell naughty stories over the port?' Beth Prickett answered pertly. 'We took a vote and decided unanimously to come and join you!'

Charles grunted. 'One hardly needs to be Sherlock Holmes to detect the hand of Megan Furzehill behind this manouevre! Come now, this has nothing to do with whether or not women should have the vote – so why attack a custom which allows the ladies to retire gracefully to the powder room?'

'Because why shouldn't we also enjoy the privilege of relieving ourselves simply by excusing ourselves from the table for a short period after the main course?' responded Megan promptly. 'It is a most unfair convention, and should be abolished along with other antiquated practices which are solely designed to treat women like second-class citizens. And now, please answer this question honestly, gentlemen. Did we or did we not interrupt a ribald tale? Still, it is up to you, Fred – you are the host – and if you wish us to leave, of course, we will bow to your wishes.'

He spread his hands and answered, 'Well, I have no strong feelings either way. Perhaps the best way to decide is to take a democratic vote, as you ladies did in the drawing-room.'

'Good idea, Fred,' I said, eyeing the superbly heaving breasts of Lady Elizabeth Prickett. 'The girls have convinced me that they should stay. What's your view, Beresford?'

'Game, set and match to Megan, I fancy,' he said with a sigh. 'Charles, has her argument also won you over?'

'I suppose so,' grumbled the good-natured impresario. 'But only on condition that we should feel quite at liberty to continue the conversation that was taking place before we were interrupted.'

Megan gave us a beaming smile and said, 'By all means, there is no need for you to feel uninhibited. Fred, is it in order for us to resume our places?'

'Of course,' he answered, and he offered Megan the decanter of port. 'I think this calls for a toast, don't you?'

On reflection, I think that Fred Nolan would rather have not continued with his anecdote, for he protested that Norma and Suzie might prefer him not to carry on with the story behind his latest film. However, the two girls made no objection and, indeed, after a whispered little conference, they announced that if we all adjourned next door, they would be pleased to act out the scene captured on film by our host.

'Of course, we only let Fred photograph us because he gave his word that the film will be screened solely in America and that, to the best of his abilities, he will not permit copies to be shown in Europe,' said Norma, as she and Suzie helped each other to unhook the clasps on their dresses. Charles picked up the gowns from the floor and laid them carefully over a chair, whilst the girls sat down on the sofa, unhitched their suspenders and peeled off their stockings, giggling away as they then stood up and pulled off their slips, to stand in only similar pairs of flimsy silk knickers.

'Suzie, I didn't know that you were also given knickers by Lord Lempert?' enquired Norma, stroking her magnificently rounded breasts, which were tipped with delightful round aureoles and exquisitely elongated raspberry nipples.

'Yes, he was a very kind gentleman,' replied Suzie, whose own nude bosoms, though not Norma's equal in size, jutted out proudly, and were capped by even larger tawney stalks that simply ached to be rubbed and sucked.

One look at Beresford's trousers showed that, like myself (and, no doubt, Fred and Charles), his prick was growing stiffer by the second. And my tool bulged uncomfortably when Suzie said, 'Rupert, would you like to help me off with my knickers?'

'And perhaps Charles would like to assist me in similar fashion?' said Norma sweetly, and the girls sat down again on the sofa.

Charles and I exchanged a knowing glance, then we stepped forward and the girls raised their bottoms invitingly. I took hold of Suzie's panties and Charles took hold of Norma's, and on Beresford's count of three, we pulled them down and over their well-shaped ankles. The girls gaily kicked these garments off their feet and in a trice they were fondling each other in a passionate embrace.

'Well, I won't have to tell you anything more about the film – you can see what I captured on my camera for yourselves,' joked our host as his arm slipped around Beth Prickett's waist.

But, like the others, my eyes were fixed upon Suzie, who was now lying down on the carpet with Norma on top of her, kissing and squeezing her jiggling breasts and then, as Suzie started to moan in delight, Norma slid her hands down and under the other girl's quivering bottom to clutch her plump bum cheeks and draw herself down until she could nuzzle her head into the flaxen fluff between Suzie's thighs. I could hear Norma's naughty tongue slurping in and out of Suzie's cunney. Then Suzie started to drum her heels on the carpet, and her body jerked fiercely up and down whilst Norma continued to suck away on her tingling pussey.

Norma lifted her mouth from the younger girl's sopping quim to take a deep breath and her lips were all shiny from her partner's cuntal juices. Then she began to massage Suzie's cunt in earnest, the knuckles of her left hand working over the erect bud of her clitty, which I could see peeking out between her wide love lips, whilst at the same time she inserted three fingers into Suzie's cunt, working them rapidly in and out of the juicy love channel. Suzie squealed with pleasure, her hips bucked up and down and she cried out, 'Norma, you wicked thing! Your fingers feel just like a big thick cock reaming out my cunney! Faster now, I want to spend!'

She continued to writhe like one demented, until she finally shuddered to a glorious climax and lay still, gasping for breath. Now Norma withdrew her fingers, coated with pungent love juice, and smeared the sticky essence on Suzie's swollen nipples. She hauled herself back on top of the trembling girl so that their soft, slippery bodies were now glued to each other with their breasts and cunnies mashed together.

'Suzie, I am now going to fuck you,' Norma panted breathlessly – words which puzzled me, for how could she do this without a dildo? But I found out the answer when I craned my head down to see her open the blonde girl's pussey lips with her fingers and direct her own protruding stiff clitty into Suzie's slit, before closing her cunney lips with her hand to complete an exciting erotic conjunction.

'Is that nice? Can you feel my clitty inside your cunt?' gasped Norma as she rocked to and fro, and was rewarded by a series of throaty little gurgles from Suzie, who obviously enjoyed being poked in this novel fashion.

It was most arousing to see their delicious backsides wobbling like jellies as the two nude girls rolled around from side to side. Although I was quite unprepared when, to my complete astonishment, Norma suddenly called out, 'Well, don't just stand there like a spare prick at a wedding, Rupert Mountjoy! Get undressed and come and join us – I want your meaty cock in my cunney as soon as possible!'

I was so surprised by this earthy request that I stood stock-still until Megan Furzehill snapped her fingers in front of my face, saying in a commanding tone of voice, 'You heard what she said, Rupert! Hurry up now and oblige the lady.'

To a round of applause led by my cousin Beresford, she helped me tear off my clothes, and encouraged me even further when I had tugged down my drawers by taking hold of my throbbing tool and slicking her hand up and down my stiff shaft, as I took up position and sank to my knees behind Norma, who thrust out her tight little rump to greet the arrival of Mr Pego. Megan released my todger to part Norma's ravishing bum cheeks and reveal her wrinkled little rear dimple. However, I was more interested in a 'doggie-style' shag than a bottom-fuck, so I lifted Norma's arse (which of course caused her clitty to slip out of Suzie's cunt) to effect an easy lodgement for my pulsating prick. This stratagem worked well, for my cock now slid inside Norma's dripping love crack with the utmost ease.

And what a blissful fuck this turned out to be! Waves of ecstatic abandon swept through me as I pumped my sturdy shaft in and out of Norma's squelchy love tunnel, whilst the friction of this fuck at the same time frigged Suzie's pussey quite brilliantly. So I gave both girls the benefit of my trusty tool and this thought was so arousing that I reached the summit of the mountain of desire more quickly than I would have liked, although I could almost feel my balls lighten as I squirted jet after jet of frothy white jism into Norma's sopping cunt.

'Oh dear, I'm afraid that was all rather too fast for you,' I apologised as I withdrew my glistening wet semi-erect cock, but the girls assured me that they had both achieved an orgasm.

'You performed very well and I think the two of us should reward your clever cock with a good sucking,' said Norma warmly and Suzie nodded her pretty head in agreement, adding sweetly, 'You would like us to suck your prick, wouldn't you?'

I felt it unnecessary to reply and simply smiled glassily at her. Then I turned my head to see that Megan Furzehill was now in her underwear and helping Fred Nolan to tear off his clothes. Lady Beth Prickett and Beresford were both naked, my cousin sitting in a chair with his cock standing stiffly to attention. Beth was sitting over him, about to spit herself upon his thick upright weapon.

This had left poor Charles Viney out in the cold, and so I cleared my throat and suggested that instead the two lusty young trollops should pay attention to the impresario's straining shaft, which was threatening to burst out of his trousers.

'How thoughtful of you to think of your friend,' said Suzie approvingly. 'Strip off, Charles, and Norma and I will palate your prick whilst Rupert has a well-deserved rest.'

He obeyed in double-quick time and lay down next to me as the giggling little minxes climbed all over him. Norma jammed down his foreskin to expose the smooth velvety dome of his helmet, then motioned to the younger girl that she should have the pleasure of the first suck of this succulent sweetmeat.

Suzie sucked deeply, letting Charles's bell-end slide against her cheek whilst her lips smacked together as she lubricated his thick veiny shaft. Then she pulled her head upwards so that only his knob remained between her lips and she licked and lapped around the ridges of his helmet whilst Norma tongued the underside of his love truncheon, which made him let out pulsing gasps of pleasure.

Seeing that he was in imminent danger of shooting his load, Suzie set free his cock from its thrilling imprisonment inside her mouth, and then Norma transferred her attentions to my own palpitating prick, which was soon as stiff as a poker again when she began to nibble all around the wide crown of my cock before starting to suck it in earnest.

Norma proved herself to be a most skilled fellatrice, for she gobbled my shaft quite beautifully, bobbing her head up and down in a way which sent me into a wild frenzy of sensual joy. And to ensure that I did not spend too quickly, each time she felt my balls hardening, she immediately released my throbbing tool so as to prolong her delectable ministrations.

Meanwhile, Suzie had climbed over Charles, and I saw her pull open her cunney lips and teasingly rub her pussey along the top of Charles's prick before she took mercy upon him and plumped herself down upon his straining shaft. Now, some girls are slightly unsure as to how best sit upon a vertical cock, but this nubile nineteen-year-old rode the impresario with great assurance, jamming his cock inside her sopping cunney and bumping up and down on his delighted member. With some effort, Charles grasped hold of her thrilling young body and pulled her downwards so that he could lick her erect tawney nipples. This sent Suzie wild and she thrashed from side to side as she felt the approach of her climax, and then Charles let out a low growl and sent a torrent of spunk streaming into her cunney to mingle with her own flood of love juices, and she shouted with glee as his copious emission flooded into her, draining his balls dry.

I began to jerk my hips up and down, but Norma now wrenched her lips away and, to my surprise, she clambered to her feet and padded across to where Megan Furzehill was on her knees between Fred Nolan's thighs, lustily sucking his big balls whilst she fisted her clenched hand up and down his truly enormous stiffstander.

Incidentally, our genial host is of slim build

and, if anything, under average height. Watching Megan masturbate him, it occurred to me that the size of his tremendous todger proved once again that there was truth in the old maxim that the smallest jockeys carry the biggest whips!

Be that as it may, Norma whispered into Megan's ear and the feisty dark-haired girl nodded and, releasing Fred's wrinkled scrotum from her mouth, hauled herself up to her feet. However, before he had time to protest at this interruption, Norma dropped down on her knees to take Megan's place and gulped in Fred's twitching tool between her lips. I watched Megan make her way towards me.

She lay down next to me and with a twinkle in her eye she said simply, 'Norma and I would like to play Swopsies, Rupert – do you know, I've always fancied a fuck with you, but somehow I've never managed to get around to it. I hope you might feel the same way about me.'

Her directness acted as a spur and I had time only to blurt out that it would be an honour to fuck the luscious girl before she threw her arms around my neck and our lips met in a passionate kiss that made me tremble all over. We explored each other's mouths with our probing tongues, and as Megan pressed her lips even harder against mine, my fingers slid downwards to stroke through the thatch of dark curly pussey hair. I rubbed my forefinger along the length of her moistened slit, and her body began to shake with excitement as my thumb found the rubbery ball of her clitty and I broke off our kiss to move my face down to her warm breasts, making her groan with desire as I traced tiny circles around her elongated raspberry nipples with the tip of my tongue.

'Fuck me, Rupert!' Megan murmured, opening her legs wide, and my hand ran over the soft wetness of her open crack whilst I raised myself over her and, positioning my cock with my hand, guided my knob into the inviting folds of her wet, welcoming cunt.

Our bodies tumbled together as I pounded down upon her, pushing in my cock until my balls banged against her bottom as she lifted up her rear to receive the full length of my pulsating prick. Megan moved excitedly under me as my twitching chopper jerked inside her, reaming every minute fold of her juicy quim. I could see from her passionate wriggles how much she was enjoying this wonderful fuck, and sure enough she cried out, 'Rupert, how divine! I can feel my juices gushing out of my cunney! Oooh! I'm almost there. Ram your big cock in to the limit, you lovely fucker!'

I slammed my shaft in to the root and pistoned to and fro, slowing down my thrusts to prolong the pleasure and stopping occasionally to feel the exquisite throbbing of Megan's cunney muscles against my tool. Then I withdrew and drove forward again and Megan cried out as she felt my sturdy shaft fill her tingling love channel, and she wrapped her legs around my waist, holding me firmly inside her. She began to buck to and fro, her bum cheeks coming up off the carpet as I lunged into her, back and forth. Faster and faster she gyrated, until surging ripples of sheer delight engulfed me and I pumped spurt after spurt of sticky jism into her cunney whilst she achieved a tremendously exciting climax. Her thighs pressed my sides like a vice and she shrieked out her joy as a convulsive orgasm shuddered through her quivering body, and with a final surge I emptied myself into her slippery wet cunt.

I flopped down beside her, completely exhausted by the fray, looking up to see Beresford about to mount Lady Beth Prickett on the sofa. She had her fingers clutched around his gleaming shaft which she guided into the red chink between her pouting pussey lips. Beresford's body moved in furious rhythm, faster and faster, pounding his thick tool into her willing love box, until the sofa appeared in real danger of toppling over. Beth bounced up and down, screaming for satisfaction as my cousin forced his tool into the deepest recesses of her juicy cunt and she threw her legs over his shoulders to absorb every last inch of cock inside her.

'A-r-g-h! I'm off to fuckland!' Beth yelled out, and then her body went limp as Beresford withdrew his glistening swollen shaft from her cunney and she leaned forward to take his gleaming uncapped knob between her lips. Somehow she managed to gulp his entire shaft into her mouth without gagging until his hairy balls dangled in front of her straining lips to allow him to squirt jets of hot spunk down her throat. She swallowed his salty seed with relish, squeezing his balls and milking his cock until it began to lose its stiffness and Beresford pulled his deflated shaft out of her mouth.

Despite my previous exertions, my cock began to stir as I watched this libidinous scene unfold, and I idly remarked to Megan on how arousing it could be to watch another couple fuck themselves silly. She agreed with a merry laugh and said, 'I've never really given it much thought, but you are quite correct, looking at a lascivious scene does make me feel extremely randy. Why, only the other day I came home to find my flatmate Christine entwined with Sir David Kent on the settee. They were kissing each other with great passion and Sir David had Chrissie's naked breasts in his hands whilst she was rubbing her hand over the huge bulge in his trousers.

'The horny pair were so engrossed that they hadn't heard me come in, but watching them embrace made me so excited that when Sir David threw up Chrissie's skirts and pulled down her knickers, I stepped forward and unbuttoned his trousers, took out his thick cock and proceeded to suck him off. Afterwards, Sir David took the pair of us to bed and fucked us both quite beautifully in his own inimitable style.'

'Do you often fuck *à trois*?' I enquired.

'Not all the time,' Megan replied, 'but an occasional threesome can be great fun. I enjoy any computation of the sexes, but I suppose that two girls and one man makes the ideal combination. However, I'm not too bothered, as long as I am promised the use of at least one stalwart thick prick. However, on the other hand –'

Fred Nolan's voice cut in: 'There is nothing to beat a straightforward fuck, though I suppose now you will think me something of a fuddy-duddy.'

Megan and I looked up to see the sinewy figure of our host standing above us, his massive shaft rising stiffly up against his flat belly from the nest of curly dark hair under which dangled a pair of heavy looking balls in their wrinkled pink sack.

'So long as one does not become hidebound, there's nothing wrong with many of the traditional orthodoxies,' Megan commented seriously. 'For instance, whilst I like to ring the changes when fucking, I particularly enjoy being taken from behind. But for sheer comfort, I'm sure that both of you will agree that the dear old-fashioned missionary position cannot be beaten.'

'It would be an honour to fuck you in that particular style,' said Fred huskily and Megan returned his questing gaze with an easy smile, and replied, 'By all means. Besides what I have seen tonight, I remember seeing you fuck Rosie d'Argosse in one of the bedrooms at Sir William Hedworth's party at the Savoy Hotel last year. I've heard it said that her cunney muscles can nip and squeeze so tightly that she can clamp a man's cock like a vice inside her pussey.'

With a smile, Fred murmured as he slid his hand up and down his giant boner, 'It is quite true that Miss d'Argosse does have a lovely clinging cunt, but I am sure that after experiencing the joys of your own dear little quim, I will feel that, in comparison, fucking Rosie was like lobbing a jug of cream into the new Blackwall Tunnel.'

'A most unfair statement, sir,' said Megan as she lifted a hand to fondle his rampant rod. Then she sighed and went on, 'But as they say, flattery will get you everywhere . . .'

Fred gave a hearty chuckle and moved on top of Megan, whilst she gently continued to frig his pulsing stiffstander. Then slowly, as she piloted his prick into her sopping cunney, he sank down upon her soft curves and she writhed with genuine arousal as his cock twitched excitedly inside her tingling crack. She felt Fred's lips upon hers and almost at once his lean, muscular body began to rock in rhythm as he worked his quivering cock in and out of her juicy sheath.

Megan rolled from side to side, lifting her hips to meet his urgent thrusts as he plunged in and out of her sated cunt. He fucked her vigorously with long, sweeping strokes until she let out a tiny whimper and, concerned that she was not fully enjoying the fuck, he immediately pulled out his veiny shaft until only the tip of his purple knob was rubbing against her cunney lips.

'Oh Fred, I'm so sorry, but my poor pussey is becoming rather sore,' she apologised unhappily. 'I don't think I can take any more cock for a while, but perhaps you will let me finish you off by sucking your prick?'

'By all means,' said Fred, and he scrambled up

to place his glistening stiff shaft in front of Megan's mouth. She grasped hold of his cock and kissed the smooth helmet before her tongue flicked out to lick up the little pool of pre-spend cum which had already formed around the 'eye' on top of his knob.

Megan sucked his thick tool into her mouth, taking its entire ramrod length by letting it slide easily down over her tongue like a sword-swallower takes a lethal weapon between his lips. Then Fred gave a heavy grunt as, with his cock now totally hidden inside Megan's mouth, he rolled the girl over on her side whilst he lay next to her to take up a voluptuous *soixante-neuf* position. His head was now buried in her hairy bush, and I saw his long tongue track sensuously down from her belly-button through the silky foliage of pussey hair to begin licking the pouting cunney lips of Megan's cunney, which were already open to this welcome visitor. Megan let out a happy yelp when the tip of Fred's tongue rubbed over the sensitive bud of her clitty, then delved ever deeper into the moist delights of her pungent cunney.

Still holding Fred's twitching tool clamped between her lips, she moaned as Fred continued to arouse her pussey by lapping up her tangy love juices, and her hips bucked even faster until her body convulsed as crashing waves of orgasm surged through her and an abundant libation of Megan's love juice filled Fred's mouth whilst he struggled to hold the quivering girl during the repeated shudders of her passion.

When the orgasm finally subsided, ever so slowly she released his still-charged cock from her mouth and lay beside him. He also lay still and they cuddled together until her hand reached out to cradle his balls. Shivering slightly, she kissed him lightly on the tip of his gleaming wet penis and said brightly, 'Fred, darling, I'm pleased that you haven't spent yet because my quim is now quite refreshed from your tonguing, so please feel free to finish this fuck in my cunt.'

This was an invitation not to be refused! Megan lay on her back and Fred pulled her long white legs apart and she gave a final rub to his twitching tool before, with a robust thrust, he inserted his shaft to the hilt, his balls flopping against her bum. Then he slowly withdrew and slowly pushed forward inch by inch until his prick was embedded inside her clinging love channel. She rotated her arse around the fulcrum of his plunging prick and purred in appreciation as he pulled out about half of his fleshy shaft before pushing forward again. He continued this delightful process until his shaft was coated with Megan's cuntal juices.

'Finish yourself off, Fred!' she gasped, and he increased the pace until, in a voice husky with lust, he panted, 'It won't be long, I can feel the spunk boiling up in my balls!'

He added his fingers to tweak her clitty and his cock seemed to vibrate as he pistoned his prick one final time in and out of her squelchy slit. With a loud cry Fred jetted his seed inside her cunt, and it mingled with the flood of Megan's love juice which overflowed from her cunney and trickled down her thighs. Megan sighed with delight as they dissolved into the glow which I have found envelops oneself and one's partner after such a prolific session of fucking and remarked, 'My goodness, Fred, I really felt you explode inside me when you spent. Has it been a long time since you enjoyed the pleasure of a jolly good fuck?'

'I'm not surprised that you noticed a certain extra release of tension,' answered our host with a heavy sigh. 'It's been almost three weeks since my old todger has made contact with a nice juicy cunney.'

I looked at him in disbelief, for Charles Viney and other gentlemen in the entertainment business had told me that the wiry American film-maker was noted for his many and varied *amours*.

'There must be an interesting story behind this enforced abstinence,' I observed, winking at Suzie, who was now sitting with my cousin on the floor, idly toying with Beresford's balls while he drank a glass of refreshing soda water. 'After all, it isn't Lent for another three weeks!'

'I hope you haven't contracted any anti-social medical problems,' said Lady Beth anxiously, but Fred shook his head and said, 'No, no, I went to Harley Street only ten days ago for my annual check-up with Doctor Jonathan Letchmore, and I'm happy to say that he gave me a clean bill of health. No, the truth of the matter is that, since I was forced to leave a certain house in

Hampstead rather more quickly than I would have liked, I have immersed myself in work and given little thought to any amusements.'

Charles Viney burst out laughing and said, 'In Hampstead, eh? I'll lay a fiver that you are referring to a house in Platts Lane, you rogue. Well, do you deny it?'

Fred shrugged his shoulders and replied, 'No, I don't deny it, but how did you know –?'

'Oh, come on, Fred! Everyone who was at the East End Milk Fund Gala Dinner saw the lady in question make a blatant pass at you – and you didn't exactly rebuff her either, did you?' rejoined Charles, wagging a reproachful finger at our host. 'Don't tell me that the lovely young Lady Gilpin's husband came home early and caught you *in flagrante delicto*?'

Before Fred could do more than nod his head, Beresford said thoughtfully, 'I've never been in such a situation, but I've often wondered what a husband would do if he found his wife in bed with another man.'

I gave a hoarse chuckle. 'Well, it all depends upon his disposition, but I suppose a shy husband would just blush and walk away.'

'Maybe. But a conscientious husband would worry that he must have been neglecting his wife,' grunted Beresford. And then Suzie chimed in wittily, 'Whilst an avaricious husband would present the lover with a bill, and a sarcastic husband would sneer at the size of his balls!'

'Ha, ha, ha! And a modest husband would think his balls looked far bigger than his own,' giggled Norma. Then Charles stroked his chin and declared, 'However, an excitable husband would take out his prick and frig himself, although a refined husband would pull a sheet over his bottom and beg him not to stop until he had spunked, when he would offer a bowl of warm water, soap and towels to the happy couple!'

Fred pursed his lips and expelled a deep breath. 'Yes, but at the time I was worried that the husband concerned would be up my arse before I could say "Jack Robinson"! Think hard and ask yourselves why an attractive woman such as Nellie Gilpin should have to look outside her marriage for a sturdy stiff prick to slip inside her pretty cunney – if her husband was a normal red-blooded gentleman who at least attempted to satisfy her needs?'

'Hell's bells, Fred! Are you telling us that Sir Horace Gilpin is a secret homosexualist?' I gasped in astonishment, for the gentleman concerned was a bluff no-nonsense sporting type, who in winter played rugger for the Charlatans, hunted with the South Herts and occasionally turned out for the Middlesex Second Eleven during the cricket season. 'I've only met Sir Horace on a handful of occasions, and soon found that we had little in common, for it was clear that he greatly disparaged "sissy" pursuits, such as literature and the arts. But he gave no impression of being limp-wristed. I think you may be trying to spin us a yarn.'

'Not all woofters behave like the late Oscar

Wilde,' Fred replied indignantly, 'and loath as I am to spread gossip, if you must know, it was none other than Nellie herself who informed me of her husband's predelictions towards members of his own sex.'

'Tut, tut, and I remember how their wedding was one of the biggest Society events a couple of years ago,' mused Beresford with interest. 'So did she tell you whether the marriage ever consummated?'

'Oh yes, after the Milk Fund Ball, Nellie invited me to take tea with her on the following day, when the unfortunate lady poured out all her troubles. She said that she had started to worry about Horace as early as their wedding night, when even before fucking her pussey, he wanted to cork her bottom with his cock. "Don't be frightened, my dear," he told her when she expressed her displeasure at such a suggestion. "You know the old Navy Motto: 'one up the bum will make them come, and a prick up the rectum won't affect 'em'." Anyhow, after only three months, he replaced the double bed with two singles, joining her under the sheets less and less as time went by. She began to be suspicious of the attention he paid to Roger, the gardener's boy, a fresh-faced lad in whose work Horace seemed to take a strangely intense interest.

'Then one day, Nellie's worst suspicions were confirmed when she wandered round to the motor house one evening. She heard noises which suggested sexual congress was taking place, and thought it might be their butler engaged in a swift knee-trembler with one of the maids. So she peered in through the window, simply to check that nothing was greatly amiss. To her horror, she was greeted by the disgraceful sight of Horace down on his knees, gobbling Roger's erect shaft, whilst the lad slewed his prick in and out of her husband's mouth. She heard Horace mumble: "Shoot your spunk, laddie!" and watched him smack his lips in delight as the boy ejaculated his seed into his mouth.'

Fred paused and downed a large draught of cognac as Norma commented, 'What a shocking state of affairs! I mean, how dreadful to find oneself in competition with the gardener's boy for your husband's attentions. You must have felt extremely sorry for the lady who, in my opinion, had every right to look elsewhere for affection.'

'Presumably she found relief from her woes with you,' I asked Fred. He smiled wanly and agreed that, after taking tea with Nellie Gilpin, the pair of them had managed to avoid the prying eyes of the servants and scuttled upstairs to her bedroom. He went on, 'Once there, we kissed and cuddled, and soon we had kicked off our shoes and our lips met and our bodies pressed together as we rolled around in a passionate embrace on the bed.

'I tore off her blouse and slid my hands underneath her chemise to tease her hard stalky titties, whilst she unbuttoned my shirt. By then, my cock was fairly bursting and she slipped her chemise over her head and rubbed her bare breasts against my chest, nipple to nipple. She had already undone her skirt to make it easier for me to pull down and then I moved my hand down to her waist so I could roll off her white silk knickers, but Nellie was now so aroused that she raised her bottom and pulled them off herself. A heartfelt sigh escaped her lips as she lay back and parted her thighs and I started to stroke her pussey lips. Then I began to finger-fuck the trembling young lady, sliding two fingers in and out of her juicy quim.

' "Mmm, that feels absolutely divine," she groaned, and I was just about to heave myself over her and substitute my aching todger for my fingers when we heard the screech of brakes and a motor-car pulled up outside the front of the house. Nellie sat up, her face white, and hissed, "Oh my God, it's Horace. I recognise the sound of his new Daimler! Quickly, Fred, gather up your clothes and hide in the wardrobe!" '

'This is beginning to sound like a scene from one of Monsieur Feydeau's French farces,' remarked Beresford, and even Fred joined in the laughter. Then he said, 'Maybe so, but I can assure you that it didn't seem very funny at the time, especially when Horace came clumping up the stairs and flung open the bedroom door. I could see through the gap between the wardrobe doors, and breathed a sigh of relief when from his cheery manner I could see that Horace had returned home in a happy alcoholic daze.

' "Hello, darling, I didn't expect you back so soon – I thought you had some business at the solicitors this afternoon," said Nellie, covering her naked body with the eiderdown. He replied, "I couldn't be bothered, my dear. Godfrey and Godfrey will have to wait until tomorrow for me to sign some new tenancy contracts. But what are you doing in bed so early in the day? Are you feeling unwell?"

' "No, I was just taking a rest after a long walk in Golders Hill Park," she answered, cunningly sweeping off the eiderdown and exposing her nude titties and pussey to her husband's gaze. "Darling, since you're home early, why don't you come and join me on the bed for a cuddle?"

'Horace's eyes gleamed as he threw off his coat and began to undress, which surprised me for, according to Nellie, he had not fucked her more than three times at most during the previous six months. However, as I hastily pulled on my socks and slipped on my pants, he sat down on the bed, unlaced his shoes and chortled, "What a splendid idea! I asked Hutchinson why he was driving so fast and he explained that with luck he would have time to poke Mrs Bridges before she started work on our dinner. Well, the news that my chauffeur was shagging our cook made me realise that lately I have rather neglected my marital duties – however, if you are too tired, it doesn't really matter."

' "Oh no, Horace, I would love you to fuck me! I'm never too tired for that!" she cried out and began to frig herself in anticipation, manipulating her hairy pussey with the fingers of one hand and rubbing her titties with the other whilst he finished undressing. Then he climbed up on top of her and a satisfied grunt from the bed signalled that he was wasting no time in giving Nellie her conjugals. I gritted my teeth as I watched his meaty shaft slide sweetly in between the pouting lips of Nellie's sopping love funnel – moistened only a few minutes earlier by my forefinger!

'So there I was, squashed between two fur overcoats in the wardrobe, and cast in the role of an unwilling spectator looking at Horace Gilpin's fat white bottom cheeks bouncing up and down as he fucked his wife. He slowed down the pace and lay still for a moment until she panted, "Don't stop! Keep on thrusting your cock inside my tight little cunney! Sod the gardener's boy, Horace, give me a good fucking instead! Come on, I know you have a big gush of spunk in your balls to squirt inside my cunt!"

'I heard the squelch of their juices as I put on my shirt and trousers, and when I peeked out again I could see from their shudderings that they were fast approaching the point of no return. Nellie squealed with pleasure as, with a heavy grunt, he shot his load into her willing love box. But after only one lunge forward, Horace scrambled on to his haunches, holding his twitching tool in his hand as he growled hoarsely, "Now you must suck me off, my dear."

'He hauled himself nearer, so as to bring the tip of his purple helmet to her face and she kissed his prick before opening her mouth wide, taking his quivering cock between her lips. I saw her pink tongue run up and down Horace's shaft and at this point, as she began to suck lustily on his balls,

I silently opened the wardrobe door and, my shoes in my hand and the rest of my clothes draped over my arm, Nellie saw me creep out of the bedroom – and even gave me a cheery wave while she continued to suck Horace's cock, which he was moving at some speed in and out of her wet mouth.'

'Well, at least you escaped being involved in what could have been a most embarrassing situation,' said Norma comfortingly.

Fred let out a heavy sigh and went on, 'Yes, indeed, and I appreciate that fact, but it was nevertheless a most frustrating experience. Quite frankly, I was almost glad that I had to shoot up to Scotland on the sleeper the next evening and begin work in Edinburgh for a wealthy Scots-born gentleman emigrant who had made a fortune in real estate in California, and who had commissioned me to make a film about his native city which he could show at his fiftieth birthday party to his family and friends.

'I was so shaken up by the business with Nellie that looking for any willing women was the last thing on my mind up there, and even when I returned to London, it took me a couple of days before I called her, to ask her if we could continue where we had left off. However, the telephone was answered by one of the servants who informed me that Lady Gilpin was spending a few days in France with the infamous Count Gewirtz of Galicia.'

Charles swigged down the rest of his drink and commented drily, 'Well, we all know what *that* means. Sir Horace couldn't have kept up the good work, or his wife wouldn't have run off to Paris to be fucked by Johnny Gewirtz.'

'Very true, my friend,' acknowledged Fred, pouring another generous measure of cognac into Charles's crystal glass. 'And from what I heard only yesterday, none other than Lady Nellie Gilpin was a star performer at one of the Count's special soirées.'

'Oh, is the gobbling Galician still throwing wild parties?' I asked, with some interest, for I kept in touch with all the news from Paris through my regular correspondence with Diana Wigmore [see An Edwardian Dandy I: Youthful Scandals – Editor], who was now in her final year of studies at the Sorbonne, and who kept me informed of the more outrageous gossip surrounding la vie Parisienne. 'I understood that the old reprobate had stopped his monthly orgies after an unfortunate accident when he tried to take on three showgirls from the Moulin Rouge at the same time and dislocated his left knee.'

The fond remembrance of a particularly wonderful fuck I had enjoyed eighteen months before, after a fancy dress ball organised by Count Gewirtz at the Savoy Hotel in honour of His Majesty King Edward VII's sixty-fourth birthday, transmitted fresh energy into my crestfallen cock, and as it began to waken into new life, Suzie whispered into my ear, 'Rupert, I do hope you will not think me too forward, but Norma has just been telling me that you would score high marks in any examination of lovemaking. Now, whilst I

110

have no reason to distrust her judgement, I would really appreciate the opportunity to test out her theory for myself.'

'Please feel free to do so, although I cannot claim such wide experience in *l'art de faire l'amour* as Count Gewirtz or other well-known cocksmen who have fucked their way through Western Europe,' I said modestly, scrambling to my feet.

'That is of no importance – it is quality rather than quantity which matters,' murmured the slender nineteen-year-old, as she ran her fingertips lightly over my body, before cupping my balls in her cool hands. In response, I brushed my palm against her nipples, which swelled up to hard tawney bullets as I rubbed them between my fingers. Onwards and downwards I pursued my exploration and as I traced out the slight curve of her tummy, she put her arms around my neck, pulled me to her and kissed me on the lips, pressing her soft body against mine, crushing my throbbing erect tool between our bellies.

Suzie's hands now wandered up and down my sides whilst I fondled the firm-fleshed cheeks of her delicious bottom. Then, without warning, she suddenly slipped a finger into my back passage. I gasped with the shock and my cock responded immediately with a convulsive shudder. Reaching down, she slid her long fingers around my shaft and guided my bell-end towards the slightly parted lips of her cunney and I felt the silky dryness of her fluffy bush give way to the damp promise of a forthcoming entry. Rubbing herself against me, she continued to massage my knob against the entrance to her yielding crack.

Then she slowly lifted one leg and, with the elegance of a ballerina, gracefully hooked it around my waist. At once my prick slid easily into her moist quim. As I pressed my prick deeper inside her, Suzie carefully linked her hands behind my neck and swayed back to look at me at arm's length, and with a sensuous smile, observed, 'How strong are you, Rupert? Let's see if you can lift me.'

I guessed what Suzie had in mind and gritted my teeth. She pulled herself to me and raised her other leg, so that both were locked around my waist as she impaled herself completely upon my pulsing cock, which was now completely imprisoned inside her juicy cunt. A flutter of sheer bliss rippled through me as, clinging to me, Suzie nuzzled against my neck, giving a tiny sigh as she wriggled to seat herself comfortably against my thighs. 'Don't let go of me, Rupert, whatever you do!' she breathed.

Then she let go of my neck and swayed backwards, her arms hanging loosely with her fingers trailing on the carpet. I supported this delightful burden with ease, admiring the supple poise of her superb body as she slowly pulled herself back up to me and when she repeated the movement, I felt all the muscles in her back ripple under my hands. But then, as she clung to me, she lifted herself slightly, taking her weight on her arms as she pressed down on my shoulders and, her legs still locked firmly round my waist, she started to move her hips to and fro, so that her sopping love box slid up and down upon my throbbing tool.

'Oh my goodness,' I gasped, for the butterfly pressure of Suzie's clitty was now caressing my cock as it rubbed its way along the length of my slippery shaft. She began to rotate her hips and her cunney seemed to widen about me in her mounting excitement, but she possessed an amazing muscular control and she slowed down the pace, clung close for a second or two and then yelled out uninhibitedly, 'Now then, Rupert, move your bum and fill my cunt up with your hot sticky cream!'

I caught her rhythm and jerked my hips back and forth, stroking my cock in and out of her clingy cunney, faster and faster as I quickly built up to a spend and with a hoarse shout, called out that I was about to shoot my seed into her receptive wet cunt. Panting with pleasure as the muscles of her love funnel tightened wonderfully around my tingling prick, I let out a heartfelt sigh, and with a gigantic *woosh*! the first squirts of my seething emission burst out of my knob, but I continued to drive my shaft to and fro until Suzie cried out in joy as she also climaxed, shuddering all over in the glorious ecstasy of a shattering orgasm.

We tumbled down together on to the carpet in a tangle of entwined limbs to a round of applause led by our host. Naturally, my prick slipped out of Suzie's cunt as we fell, and Lady Beth Prickett sat herself down next to us. With a twinkle in her eye, she seized hold of my lubricated semi-stiff shaft and declared, 'Rupert, it would be hardly fair if I were the only lady not to be fucked by you this evening.' I smiled glassily at her as Beth continued to stroke my glistening chopper, saying, 'Your cock appears to be somewhat in need of revitalisation – but that is of no matter, I shall be pleased to lick it into shape.'

To be quite candid, even after summoning up my last reserves of mental and physical strength, I doubted if I had the ability to oblige the randy girl, but when she lowered her head and gulped in my knob between her lips, I closed my eyes and relaxed and, sure enough, after just two or three passes with her tongue and a judicious squeeze of my balls, my cock was once more fully erect.

'That's much better,' Beth said with satisfaction, and she pulled me by my cock towards the nearest armchair. She fairly threw herself over the wide padded arm so that her creamy, dimpled bum cheeks stuck proudly up in the air and called out, 'Go on, Rupert, I'm ready for you.'

I took a deep breath and guided my stiff but aching cock into the crevice between her buttocks and my knob squelched its way into her dripping quim. She pushed back her bum and forced her cunney along the full extent of my shaft, and at once we fell into a completely abandoned bout of fucking. As I slammed my shaft time and again inside her, a trickle of perspiration slithered down her back and into her bottom, but still I slewed my tired member in and out of her wet cunney.

My balls felt full to bursting and though I

attempted to delay the ultimate pleasure, very soon I experienced a contraction in my sorely tried balls and quickly exploded into a climactic release. However, only a feeble rivulet of jism gushed out from my knob into Beth's cunt and waves of fatigue coursed through me. My shaft softened, I lapsed into near unconsciousness and I slid slowly but inexorably down on to the carpet in a state of complete and utter exhaustion.

I heard Charles Viney remark, 'Poor old Rupert, I'm afraid he has fucked himself dry. Best put a pillow under his head and let him sleep it off. Lady Prickett, you didn't spend, did you? Well, if you care to come over here, I will happily finish you off in whichever manner you prefer – my tongue and my cock are at your disposal.'

'How very kind of you, Charles,' replied Beth warmly. 'Please don't be offended, but I would rather one of the girls bring me to a climax by licking out my pussey. I have yet to meet a man who can perform cunnilingus as delicately as the female of our species.'

At another time, I would have sprung to the defence of my own sex, for, without wishing to sound boastful, I have on several occasions been highly commended for my skill at 'muff diving', as the common vernacular has it, by several ladies – and not only in this country, but in France also, where the art of tonguing a lady's pussey is more widely practised. But alas, I was unable to do more than croak out a few words of protest before falling into a much-needed deep slumber.

CHAPTER THREE

Looking Up Some New Friends

WHEN I WOKE UP AT a quarter past ten the next morning in my own bed, I must admit that I possessed only the haziest recollection of what had occurred after I had collapsed whilst fucking Lady Beth Prickett. As I yawned and stretched out my arms, vague scenes of Beresford and Fred helping me on with my clothes and of me leaning on Charles's arm whilst we waited for his chauffeur to bring round the car to take us home crossed my mind, and I assumed my kind friend had assisted Edwards in putting me to bed when we arrived back at Bedford Square.

The servants had enough good sense not to wake me with the usual early morning cup of tea, although Edwards had left a neatly folded copy of the *Daily Chronicle* next to the clock on the bedside table. I picked up the paper and scanned the headlines. There was little news of interest to me, although I was delighted to read that the weather forecast was for a bright early Spring day in the London area.

'A quick bite of breakfast and then a stroll in the

park will be just the ticket,' I muttered to myself, throwing off the covers and walking to the windows where, sure enough, rays of sunlight were pouring through the gap in the curtains. I pulled them back and let the sparkling sunshine flood the room, then padded barefoot into the bathroom. Surprisingly, even though I felt somewhat jaded from my sexual high-jinks the previous evening, I was suffering no ill-effects after the liberal amount of alcoholic refreshment I had imbibed, and I made a mental note to telephone Frederick Nolan after breakfast and thank the American film-maker again for his generous hospitality.

He sounded as bright as a button when I called him up. 'Glad you enjoyed yourself, old chum,' he said, after I had expressed my gratitude. 'Have you fully recovered from your post-coital fatigue? If it's any consolation, the girls were full of praise for the way you fucked all four of them last night. But take a word of advice from an old campaigner – even for a well-endowed chap like yourself, it can't be clever to drive yourself to a state of near collapse.'

I agreed with him. 'You're absolutely right, Fred. Without doubt, the attempt to poke Lady Beth Prickett "doggie-style" was a fuck too far, but one hesitates to refuse such an attractive lady.'

'That's quite understandable, but think back on the advice our mutual friend Doctor Letchmore gave you last year, after you became worried that your prick was losing some of its potency,' [*see*

117

An Edwardian Dandy IV: Country Matters – *Editor*] counselled my mentor. 'Didn't you tell me that you're going up to Aintree for the Grand National? It might be a good idea to give your cock a complete rest until you get there. Believe me, Rupert, you will feel like a new man.'

'More like a new woman,' I answered, which made him chuckle heartily. Then I went on, 'Seriously, though, I'm sure it would make sense to take heed of the good doctor's admonition. When all is said and done, I need to be fighting fit for Amber – she wouldn't take it kindly if I greeted her with a limp prick dangling between my legs!'

'Good lad,' said Fred approvingly. 'Have a good time and I hope you back the winner.'

I thanked him again for the party, and as I put down the telephone, Edwards came in with two envelopes on his tray. 'Just two letters in the first post, sir,' he said as he proffered them to me. The larger one was a sealed brown envelope, and one look at the typewritten label and Chelsea postmark was enough to tell me that it contained my monthly copy of *The Cremorne* [*one of the rudest of the illicit underground magazines – Editor*] and I resolved to slip it into my travelling case and take it with me to read on the train when I travelled up North for the big race.

The other letter had a French stamp, and from the writing I knew it came from dear Diana Wigmore, but I decided not to waste the rest of the morning by staying indoors, so I stuffed it into my pocket and told Edwards to fetch my hat and coat as I was going to take a short constitutional in Regent's Park and would return for luncheon at half past one.

'Very good, sir, but shall I first telephone for a taxi-cab?' he asked. I told him not to bother, as there were always plenty of cabs waiting for custom at the rank around the corner in Tottenham Court Road. In fact, I did not even have to take the three-minute walk to the cab rank, because as Edwards shut the front door behind me, a taxi came to a halt less than twenty yards away. I sauntered up to it as the previous passenger, a plump gentleman in a black bowler hat, paid off the driver.

'There you are, cabbie,' said this gentleman cheerily, and as he brushed by me, I noticed that he had a rather smug, self-satisfied look on his face.

Well, as Miss Ella Wheeler Wilcox sagely wrote: 'laugh and the world laughs with you, weep and you weep alone', I thought to myself as I climbed into the cab and, settling myself in my seat, instructed the driver to take me to the bandstand at Regent's Park.

'Certainly, Mr Mountjoy,' came back the reply and my eyes opened wide. I sat bolt upright and spluttered, 'Hell's bells, how the deuce do you know my name?'

The driver let out a loud guffaw as our line of traffic was halted by a policeman at the busy junction with Store Street. He turned round and said, 'Don't you recognise me, Rupert? It's only ten years ago since we played footer together on the playing fields of St Lionel the Valiant's Academy for the Sons of Gentlefolk.'

My jaw dropped when he took off his cap. 'Good heavens,' I exclaimed loudly, 'it's Paul Hayes! Paul, what the devil are you doing driving a taxi-cab?' Then I slapped my knee as I recalled how my former classmate in the Upper Sixth had always been known for his impish sense of humour (which included sending a postal order for a copy of *The Cremorne* to be delivered to the school chaplain, the Reverend Percy Clarke, after he had delivered yet another of his sermons against the evils of 'the solitary vice').

'No, you don't need to answer – this is one of your famous practical jokes,' I said with a confident grin, but he immediately rejoined, 'Oh, I only wish it were, Rupert. But the simple fact of the matter is that if I don't drive this wretched vehicle around London six days a week I won't be able to pay off my debts.' There was an indignant toot from behind us and Paul swivelled round to see that a policeman was waving us on. With some grinding of the gears, he pulled forward.

'Can you hear me, Paul?' I called out over the sound of the engine. 'Listen, when we get to the bandstand, park the blessed cab and let's have a coffee at the little restaurant there.'

Fortunately, for a change, the weather forecast in the newspaper was totally accurate, and it was warm enough for my erstwhile driver and fellow Old Ashdonian (our school was situated on the edge of Ashdown Forest in Kent) and myself to sit outside. After I had ordered coffee and biscuits, I asked him bluntly what circumstances had led him to being forced to drive a London taxi-cab to earn his daily bread.

'Paul, I don't wish to pry, but your people are out in India, are they not? Could you not contact them for assistance?' I enquired gently, but he shook his head and said, 'Not really, Rupert. You see, the old family fortunes took a nasty fall during my last year at St Lionel's, and shortly afterwards, my father sank practically every last penny left from my grandfather's estate into a rundown tea plantation about fifty miles from Madras – the whole family except for myself now live over there. I know that things are still tight for them and I wouldn't want to give my parents any further cause for concern.'

'Oh dear, I am so sorry,' I murmured.

Paul shrugged as the waitress placed our order on the table and went on, 'All the result of some unwise speculation on the Stock Market, I'm afraid. But it's not that I was robbed of a chance to take up a place at one of the 'Varsities. As you might remember, my prowess lay more on the playing field.'

'Well, I certainly recall how you took five wickets and then scored eighty-eight not out to win the match against Marlborough – the first time we ever beat them at cricket, thanks to your single-handed sterling efforts, as Dr Keeleigh said at assembly the next day. However, surely, the Old Ashdonians Society tried to find you employment in the City after you left St Lionel's – it really shouldn't have proved too difficult a task

121

for an all-round sportsman like yourself.'

'Indeed, the old boy network came up trumps, and I secured a position as a trainee financial advisor at Perkupp's, a private merchant bank in Cheapside. Perhaps you have come across it?'

'No, I don't think so,' I said thoughtfully. 'But presumably it would be run by a relative of Roland Perkupp, who was captain of hockey when we were in the Upper Sixth.'

Paul nodded as he munched on a garibaldi biscuit, and answered with a trace of bitterness in his voice. 'His great uncle, Sir Herbert Perkupp, as a matter of fact. At first, all went quite swimmingly. The job wasn't too well-paid, but by being careful, I could just about scrape by. I didn't feel ill-used though, for in the meantime, I was learning the business. But alas, my downfall began last summer.' He paused and pursed his lips, staring silently down at the table whilst his hands pressed tight around his coffee cup.

I reached out and gently patted his arm, saying quietly, 'What happened, old boy? Of course, you don't have to tell me, but if you do, I promise that I'll keep anything you say in the strictest confidence.'

'So long as you keep it to yourself, Rupert, I don't mind telling you what happened,' he replied, and raised his head to look me straight in the eye, then added with some vehemence, 'I was dismissed in disgrace from the bank – but whilst I may have acted like a bloody fool, I swear to you on my honour as an Old Ashdonian that I did nothing remotely dishonest, and if it takes me fifty years, I am determined to clear my name.'

'I'm sure you didn't,' I said soothingly. 'Tell me exactly what occurred last summer, for, whilst I won't make any promises, if you have been falsely accused, I will help you fight your corner in any way I can.'

Paul looked at me gratefully and said, 'Thank you for your trust, Rupert, and I'll hold nothing back from you. Well, life began to go sour on me last July, when I stupidly began a romantic attachment to a stunning young girl in the offices of the bank. She was an assistant cashier and her name was Julia Brenton, a lovely rosy-cheeked lass not yet eighteen years old, who always seemed to have a smile on her lips when she spoke to me. Now, I didn't know any girls in London and frankly, even if I had been involved with another, I would still have been flattered by the attention Julia showed me. At first, I was too shy to ask her out, for I was convinced that such an attractive creature was certain to have a beau. But at last, one day, I finally plucked up courage to ask her out for supper, and I was absolutely delighted when she accepted my invitation.

'We had a lovely time and at the end of the evening, as we shook hands on the doorstep of the small house in Clerkenwell where Julia lived with her parents, she immediately agreed to see me again after work the very next night. I took her to the music hall and then – as the Alhambra is very near my own lodgings off High Holborn – whilst we streamed out of the theatre, I daringly asked her if she would come back to my rooms for tea.

' "Yes, I'd love to," she said, and five minutes later she was sitting on the settee in my living-room. I asked if she preferred tea or perhaps a cold drink, for the weather had been very warm, and I had kept bottles of mineral water and lemonade in my small ice-box.

' "Lemonade would be lovely," she replied, then she took hold of my hand and motioned me to sit down next to her. "It was almost oppressively hot in the theatre, wasn't it?" she said. "Yes, it was far too warm, I would liked to have taken off my jacket," I said, and Julia smiled and said with a gay laugh, "Silly boy, you mustn't be frightened to defy convention. Now I come to think of it, I am still feeling so warm that, not only am I going to remove my jacket, I am going to take off all my clothes."

'I could not believe what I had just heard, but Julia stood up and, after swiftly unbuttoning her dress, she slipped it off and let it fall to the ground. Then, dressed only in her underwear, she sat down on the settee and peeled off her stockings, all the time looking at me closely in a knowing and confident manner.

' "Why don't you do the same?" she enquired brightly, standing up again. And then, with her back to me, she swept off her chemise over her head. She turned to face me and I nearly fainted with emotion when I looked at her youthful bouncy breasts, each tipped with the most mouth-watering large raspberry nipples which I ached to squeeze in my hands.

' "Hurry up, Mr Hayes, take off your clothes,"

124

she repeated, a sensuous smile playing about her lips. Then she tugged down her pink cotton knickers and stood in glorious nudity before my very eyes.

'Now I moved at the speed of sound, and rapidly disrobed, and as soon as I had yanked down my drawers, Julia took three quick paces towards me, planted her hands on the sides of my face and gently kissed me on the lips. I was still in a state of shock and barely responded when this delectable girl kissed me a second time, but when she drew breath for a third kiss, my arms went round her neck, my cock shot up in salute to press between our bellies, and my tongue snaked between her teeth as our mouths locked together in a burning embrace.

'I let go of her and took a step backwards to drink in her naked beauty. Rupert, you may take my word for it, this girl was one of the most beautiful I have seen, either before or indeed since that moment. Her pretty face shone with the bloom of a girl whose eighteenth birthday was still three months away. Slender in figure, she was blessed with firm, proudly uptilted breasts, a flat tummy, narrow waist and long tapering legs between which nestled a fluffy grove of silky light brown hair.

' "Where is your bedroom?" she whispered, and when I jerked my head to the door on my left, she took my hand and led me towards it. Once inside, we embraced again and fell upon the bed together and moments later I felt Julia's mouth and tongue begin a grand tour of my body, licking and lapping every inch of me until the tip of her pink little tongue played around the top of my uncapped helmet.

'She stroked my shaft and my cock leaped crazily in her hand as she rested her head on my thigh and started to suck on my knob, washing her wet tongue around the ridges before sliding it slowly down the sensitive underside. Then, to my great delight, she let her tongue slip over my balls and run deliciously along the passage between my scrotum and arsehole – this simply drove me wild and my whole body began to shake. Sensing that I was in danger of spending too soon, Julia transferred her wicked tongue back to my knob, flicking at it so expertly that my balls began to tighten and I gasped out wordlessly with passion.

' "Now I want you to fuck me," she murmured softly, after giving my knob one final lathering, and she lay on her back with her legs apart, and I could see her pink love lips jutting through the hairy blanket which surrounded the entrance to her cunney. With a strangled cry I leaped upon her and sank my rigid tool into the warm moist softness of her cunt, and the walls of her love channel clamped around my prick as I lay still, my twitching shaft totally embedded inside her.

'Then I started to slide my cock to and fro, and raised myself upon my knees so that I could grind my rock-hard member against the swelling bud of her clitty. Faster and faster, I pumped in and out of her juicy quim, until she gasped, "Oh! Oh! That's gorgeous, Paul! What a lovely big cock you have, I can feel every inch of it reaming out my pussey. Oooooh, I'm almost there already! Keep fucking me, you randy rascal, you can fill my cunney with spunk any time you like.''

'On hearing that Julia's climax was so near, I pressed my finger against her clitty and held my cock inside her cunt as she began to spend, shivering and trembling all over as spasm after spasm shook her lovely body, and I felt her cunney grip my cock even harder as she entered the throes of orgasm. She screamed out her pleasure and clasped my bum cheeks in her hands as I resumed thrusting my shaft in and out of her cunt. Almost at once I exploded into her, and a torrent of jism erupted out of my prick, filling her love box to the brim with my copious emission.'

Despite himself, Paul smiled wryly at the recollection and added, 'Rupert, I've enjoyed a reasonable amount of pussey since we left school, but I can tell you that I have never experienced a more delightful fuck. I brought in glasses of cold lemonade and we lay there talking for about half an hour before Julia caught sight of the time and said she had to leave straightaway or her parents would be very angry with her. So we hurriedly dressed ourselves and I blew another one and sixpence on a passing taxi to take Julia home to Bethnal Green.

'Over the next two weeks I raided my Post Office savings account and took Julia out almost every night. Inevitably, the evening would finish with a delightful fuck in my bed or on the settee, and it appears that several other employees at

Perkupp's made comments about how I was walking around the office with a seemingly permanent smile upon my face.' He paused and finished his coffee whilst I rubbed my hand slowly down my cheek and observed that in such circumstances as Paul described, I would also have been walking on air!

But Paul's face darkened and he said gloomily, 'Perhaps so, but this happy state of affairs quickly ended one day, when Mr Perkupp himself called me into the office and handed me a sealed envelope which he told me had to be delivered by hand to Sir Sampson Boote. I said nothing, but looked at him quizzically, for such menial work as this would normally be carried out by one of our messenger boys.

'Mr Perkupp must have seen the puzzled expression on my face, for he gave a short laugh and said, "Don't worry, Mr Hayes. This does not herald any demotion or expression of disapproval at your conduct." He beckoned me to come closer, and continued in a low voice, "Indeed, I have deliberately selected you for this simple task because the task requires someone trustworthy with a disposition able to cope with a fiery-tempered gentleman like Sir Sampson.

' "Inside this envelope are irrevocable bearer bonds for ten thousand pounds [*In real terms, the equivalent of £200,000 today – Editor*] cashable in any major bank almost anywhere in the world, and I want you to give these personally to Sir Sampson – to himself alone, mind, and to nobody else – and then obtain his signature for their safe receipt. For the sake of security, obtain half a crown petty cash from Mr Batt and take a taxi to the offices of Sampson Hale International Trading in the Aldwych. You should leave immediately, as Sir Sampson, who as you know is one of our most important clients, expects these bonds to be with him inside the hour."

'I saw Julia as I came out of Mr Perkupp's office and she obviously knew of all this for she enquired whether I had been asked to give Sir Sampson Boote his bonds. When I said that I would be on my way as soon as I had picked up some money for the taxi fare, she said, "Oh, then I'll come with you, if I may, for it's almost time for my luncheon break. Let me just file these papers and then I'll meet you by the front door in five minutes."

'At first I was inclined to demur, but then thought that no harm could come by Julia accompanying me. She could wait outside whilst I transacted my business and as it was a nice summery day, we could then buy some sandwiches and eat them in the open air in Lincoln's Inn Fields before returning to work. So I agreed, but told her not to keep me waiting as I wanted to deliver the bonds as soon as possible.

' "I won't," she promised, and she was as good as her word, for after obtaining the petty cash from Mr Batt, I had to wait only about a minute by the front door for her to come down the stairs. Nevertheless, once we were outside I wanted to hail a passing taxi, but Julia took hold of my arm and kissing my ear, she said, "It's such a lovely

129

day, Paul, let's walk up to the rank. It's only a hundred yards away and I can see several cabs waiting."

'We never got to the taxi rank – two men suddenly rushed up behind us and bundled us into a small alleyway. Whilst one of the fellows pinioned my arm behind my back, the other villain, a swarthy complexioned chap with a small clipped moustache, put a revolver to Julia's head and threatened to blow out her brains and then mine if I didn't hand over the envelope.'

I clapped my hand over my forehead and exclaimed, 'My God, it sounds like a scene from a Drury Lane melodrama! What did you do?'

Paul Hayes buried his face in his hands and said quietly, 'At first, I said nothing, not out of bravery, but because I was so shocked that I could hardly take in what was happening. But then Julia cried out, "Give it to him, Paul!" and I made no attempt to resist when the man behind me released my arm and pulled me round to face him. He pulled the envelope from my pocket and before I could do or say anything I felt a sharp blow on my head and I crumpled to the ground – not fully unconscious, for I heard them running away, but I was so dazed that it took me a few moments to drag myself up and call out for assistance. But there was no one else in the alley and I staggered into Cheapside, where again I raised the alarm. Luckily (or so I thought at the time) a policeman happened to be passing and he came running up and I told him what had happened.

'Well, he took me down to the police station, which was only a few minutes' walk away, and there I repeated my story to an inspector. I wanted to go back to work, but he insisted that I stayed in his office to rest after my ordeal, whilst he went to Perkupp's and informed my employer as to what had taken place.'

I frowned at Paul and said angrily, 'Don't tell me you were dismissed simply because you were the victim of a street robbery. How very unfair – what else could you have been expected to do with a robber waving a gun in your face? It isn't as if you were flaunting a wad of five-pound notes in the air as you walked down Cheapside.'

'No, but I was seen going out with Julia,' he countered, and gave a deep sigh. 'If I had simply been dismissed for carelessness, that would have been bad enough, but much worse was to follow. The bank issued new bonds to Sir Sampson Boote, and Mr Perkupp managed to persuade the police not to publicise the affair, but during their enquiries a constable interviewed an ice-cream vendor who said he had seen two men and a girl running out of the alley at the time, but that, far from looking terrified, the girl was laughing all over her face, as were her companions.'

'Great Scott! Julia was a willing accomplice!' I gasped.

Paul smiled ruefully and said, 'Indeed she was, and we never saw her again. The police went round to her address and discovered that, far from living with her parents, she was simply lodging with a respectable family who described her as a pleasant, quiet girl who always paid her rent on time. When the police searched her room they found only a few clothes, for the night before she had packed most of her personal belongings into a trunk, which a carrier had picked up earlier on the day of the robbery. So no one has any idea where she is, or even what her real name might be – and as for the bonds, they were unnumbered and can never be traced, so it will be easy for the thieves to cash them.'

Suddenly, I realised how tragic this business must have been for my old school chum. 'I think I'm getting the picture now, Paul. Am I correct in assuming that the police started to suspect that you might have had a hand in this sorry business?'

'Exactly so, Rupert,' he answered. 'From questioning the family with whom Julia lived, as well as my own landlord, they established that Julia and I were lovers, and I did not attempt to deny that I had not hidden details of my journey to Sir Sampson Boote from her. However, they could not find any real evidence that I had been in league with her, although a team of plain clothes detectives followed me everywhere for many weeks afterwards.

'Anyhow, to conclude this unhappy tale, I was dismissed from Perkupp's without any reference, and I found it impossible to obtain any work when I applied for similar posts in other financial institutions. So I borrowed some money from a relative and obtained a licence to drive a motor-cab. The fat man you saw getting out of the taxi in Bedford Square this morning is Mr Johnstone, who owns the company for which I work, and he is a very decent sort of fellow. His brother is a former policeman who now runs a firm of private investigators, and in addition to paying off my cousin's loan, I am also saving up to hire them to track down Julia and her accomplices so that my name is cleared once and for all.'

'You poor chap,' I said sympathetically, fishing out my wallet. Paul protested that there was no way he would accept any money from me: 'I haven't sunk that low,' he said firmly.

'I wasn't going to give you any money except for the fare,' I said mildly. 'And I would like you to take my card, and I'll note down your address. Perhaps you have forgotten the Lady Jane Warren Bequest for Old Ashdonians in need of financial assistance. Now, whilst one cannot apply directly for a grant, it only needs the signature of three former pupils of St Lionel's to have a case considered by the trustees. I would be happy to make such an application on your behalf, and I am sure that I would have no difficulty in finding two other chaps to put their names to a letter. Of course, there can be no guarantee of aid from the Bequest, but I'm sure that a case like yours would receive a sympathetic hearing.'

Paul Hayes's face brightened as I spoke, and he seized my hand and shook it warmly. 'That is very kind of you Rupert. I had quite forgotten about the Lady Jane Warren Fund, and I would be most grateful if you would write a letter on my behalf.'

He pulled a pencil and a sheet of paper from his

jacket and scrawled down his address. 'This is the boarding house where I am currently lodging . . . once again, let me thank you, Rupert. It's all been such a strain that – well, between you, me and the gatepost, the landlady has let me know that if I gave her a good seeing-to, I could move into the best room at no higher rent. The poor lady was widowed at thirty-three a few years back, and normally I'd have no hesitation in giving her a poke, but since that fateful day when I was duped by Julia, my old todger has gone on strike and I don't think I'll be able to fuck again until I've managed to prove my innocence.'

'Hmm, I would try not to let business interfere with pleasure,' I said thoughtfully, pushing two shillings across the table to him. 'Here's your fare. After all, you must face the fact that it could be years before the thieves are apprehended. Now as for your recalcitrant cock, I know a young lady living in Ealing who may be able to help you –'

But Paul's attention had been drawn to two gentlemen standing by his cab, and he rose from his seat. 'Tell me another time, Rupert, these chaps look as though they are looking for a taxi and I need to earn every penny I can. Thank you again for everything, and I look forward to hearing from you about any news from the Lady Jane Warren Bequest.'

I paid the waitress for the coffee and biscuits, stood up and decided to take a stroll round the boating lake before going home for luncheon, after which I would read Diana Wigmore's letter from Paris. As I sauntered round the edge of the lake, I thought I made out two feminine voices chattering away in the vicinity, but I paid no notice to them until I spotted a dainty patent leather shoe floating towards me on the surface of the water. It evidently had just dropped in for it was still right side up when I bent down and picked up a stick, with which I pulled it to the bank.

Then, behind me, I heard a distressed voice say in sweetly accented tones, '*Merde*, Kitty, I have lost my shoe. I was sitting on a bench taking a pebble out of the heel when I was startled by a pigeon fluttering close to my head and I dropped it – the shoe, that is, not the pebble.'

I turned round and saw a beautiful girl hopping towards me like a stork on one foot, and giving tiny yelps of protest when the other foot, clad in a delicate silk stocking, came in contact with the ground.

I took out my handkerchief and with studied ostentation polished the shoe, then, giving a little bow, I offered it to the distressed girl and said, 'I believe this shoe is yours, *mademoiselle*.'

'*Merci bien, monsieur*,' she gasped, taking it from me and, sitting hurriedly upon a bench, she took off her gloves and, raising her skirt with no undue concern, slipped on the shoe whilst I looked on with amused detachment. There was something familiar about this charming girl's face but I couldn't quite remember where I had seen her before. I puckered my lips in concentration and then snapped my fingers in glee. Unless I was dreadfully mistaken, this nubile young creature was none other than the girl whose photographs Lieutenant Andy Coles had shown me the previous day over luncheon at the Jim Jam club, and who was, according to Andy, the close companion of old Sir Bernard Barnes whose house was only ten minutes' walk away in Avenue Road, St John's Wood.

Now what the devil was her name? I racked my brains, but simply could not recall it. Well, nothing ventured, nothing gained, I said silently. And as her equally attractive companion joined her on the bench, I tipped my hat to the girls and said, '*Mademoiselle*, forgive my approaching you without an introduction, but I believe we have a friend in common who lives quite close to Regents Park.' She looked up at me questioningly and I went on, 'I am referring to Sir Bernard Barnes – would I be right that you are currently staying at his house whilst you are in London?'

Two delicious dimples formed on either side of her mouth, as with a smile she looked up at me and said, 'Yes, I have been living at his house since the beginning of the month, and will stay until he returns from Baden Baden in two weeks' time. You did not mention your name, *Monsieur*. You are –?'

'Mountjoy, Rupert Mountjoy, at your service,' I said promptly, taking her proffered hand and kissing her fingers in the Continental style.

'I am Claudia Renouvin and this is my friend and colleague Miss Kitty Forrest,' she went on. I shook hands with the English girl, murmuring, 'A pleasure to meet you, Miss Forrest. I don't think our paths have ever crossed.'

She grinned saucily up at me. 'Actually, we have met before, Mr Mountjoy, or have you forgotten the private reception given in January by friends of Lieutenant Andrew Coles at the Jim Jam Club, to celebrate his twenty-fifth birthday?'

'Were you there, Miss Forrest?' I said politely. 'Alas, it was so rowdy an affair that I'm afraid I don't remember very much about it.'

'Neither do I, but I do have a certain memory of your rendition of a comic monologue entitled 'She Was Only A Farmer's Daughter'. She spoke in honeyed tones, which caused my cheeks to burn scarlet as I attempted to cope with this discomforting information, for by the time I was called upon to recite these extremely rude verses, I had drunk too many glasses of Buck's Fizz [*the then newly popular tipple of champagne and orange juice – Editor*] to know who was in the audience listening to me.

As if she were reading my mind, the delightful girl put me at my ease by adding, 'Please don't feel concerned – I was not in the least offended. Like Claudia, I am a very broadminded person, or I would not have been at Andrew's birthday party in the first place.'

At their invitation, I sat down and during our conversation, Claudia described to me the strange circumstances which led her to be spending some time in London. It appears that she was selling programmes at the *Comédie Française* in Paris when Sir Bernard Barnes, who is easily old enough to be her grandfather, approached her and, after ascertaining that she spoke English, presented her with his card.

'He told me that he was a keen amateur photographer and would like me to model for him in London. "But why in London?" I asked, and he replied: "Because I didn't bring my best camera to Paris and not even my friend Count Gewirtz has any photographic equipment of the quality of my 1899 Kantorovitch Whole Plate camera. Less than a hundred were made by Meyer Kantorovitch before he left Odessa for America, after the rabble destroyed his workshop during a vicious pogrom in the city, and I doubt if there are more than thirty left in all Europe." *Mon Dieu*, I could hardly believe my ears when this eccentric *milord* continued: "I would like you to pose in suitable classical garb. Could you be packed and ready to leave Paris by eleven o'clock on Thursday morning?"

I nodded sagely and remarked, 'Ah, that sounds just like old Bernard. He goes blithely on his way, never deflected from obtaining what he wants by any consideration but that of his own needs. Yet his generosity is well known, and I would suspect that he offered you a handsome amount to accompany him back to London at such short notice.

Claudia smiled her agreement. 'He was *most* generous and made me an offer I simply could not refuse, and while he is taking the waters at Baden Baden with Lord Brettenham, he has left me ample funds to enjoy myself during his absence.'

As she spoke, the chimes of a Church clock

made me look at my watch – it was already half past twelve, and I asked Claudia and Kitty if they had made any arrangements for luncheon.

'Ugh, I wish you hadn't reminded us of the time,' said Kitty with a grimace. 'Claudia and I promised Bernard that we would represent him at the German Embassy this afternoon, where the famous contralto Madame Elena Zimmermann is giving a concert of seventeenth century *lieder*.'

'Yes, and a promise is a promise, so we must go,' sighed Claudia, adding with a chuckle, 'Besides, I've already bought some earplugs.'

'In that case, when would you both be free to dine with me?' I demanded, and the girls rummaged in their handbags to consult their diaries. 'Any night would suit me except for next weekend, when I am to be out of town.'

Without too much difficulty, we settled on the following Monday evening and I gave my card to the girls. Then they stood up and I raised my hat and called out, 'Look forward to seeing you,' as they scuttled away.

An unseasonable bank of low grey cloud now covered the sun and I walked briskly through the park towards Chester Gate. In Albany Road I flagged down a cab which chuntered through the traffic, depositing me outside my front door shortly after one o'clock. After a wash and brush-up, I sat down to a tasty light luncheon of macaroni soup, lamb cutlets and an apple tart prepared by Mrs Riley, the excellent new cook engaged by the formidable Mrs Harrow, Colonel Wright's housekeeper. She took care of all the domestic arrangements during my stay in his home, whilst the gallant Colonel completed his work in New Delhi for the Royal Commission on Higher Education for Natives in the Indian sub-continent.

I patted my mouth with my serviette and rose up from the table to walk to the library where I would finish my repast with a cup of black coffee and a glass of kummel, a most agreeable liqueur to which I was recently introduced by Count Gewirtz. It has a base of caraway seed and not only possesses a pleasant taste, but also aids the digestion.

'Will that be all, sir?' enquired Edwards as he held open the door of the dining-room for me.

'Yes, thank you,' I answered. 'And please pass my compliments to the cook on an excellent luncheon. Incidentally, would you also tell Mrs Riley that I think I'll dine at my Club this evening, to see if I can find myself a good partner for the bridge tournament being held there tonight.' [*By the turn of the century, auction bridge (now superseded by contract bridge) had replaced whist as the most popular card game amongst the leisured classes – Editor*]

I sank down in an easy chair and sipped my kummel, then I suddenly remembered that I had yet to read Diana Wigmore's letter, which had arrived that morning. I would be glad when her studies of the history of art at the Sorbonne had finished and she would return to England and hopefully to my bed, for although we had both agreed that we must act as free agents whilst she was in Paris, I had yet to meet a girl who could top Diana's performance between the sheets.

Be that as it may, I pulled the envelope from the inside of my jacket, slit open the envelope with my thumb in the absence of a paper knife, and settled down to read her lengthy missive, which opened as follows:

Dear Rupert,

Greetings from Gay Paree! I have been enjoying a hectic time recently – just on one day last week I attended the opening of the new exhibition of pictures by Gaugin and Van Gogh, and then after tea with Baroness Reiss at the Hotel Crillon, I dressed up for the gala dinner and dance thrown by Count Gewirtz to celebrate the fourth anniversary of the Entente Cordiale. *My social diary is now so crowded that I must confess to having neglected my studies lately – in all honesty, darling, just at the moment, life is all balls, ha, ha!*

'Now, I don't have too much time to write because I must attend Monsieur Ruelle's lecture on the Dutch Old Masters of the seventeenth century, and I know that you like to hear detailed accounts of more intimate matters, so I will come straight to the point and inform you as to what took place at about two o'clock in the morning during Count Gerwirtz's ball. I had been dancing with Major Sinclair Stevenson, the military attaché at the British Embassy, and when the music ended, I curtsied to my partner and then made my way upstairs to one of the rooms which had been set aside for the ladies.

Unfortunately, I was misdirected by one of the

141

Count's servants, and made my way towards the second room on the left at the top of the staircase, instead of the right, and in consequence, when I threw open the door I found myself in one of the guest bedrooms. Of course, if the room had been empty, my mistake would have been of little consequence, but this was not the case. For, sitting quite naked together on the bed, was none other than my host, Count Gewirtz, and an acquaintance of mine from the Sorbonne, Mademoiselle Yvette Marchand!

She is a tall girl, blessed with long tresses of strawberry blonde hair, a pretty face set off by richly pouting cherry lips and a brilliant set of pearly white teeth. But my eyes were fixed upon Yvette's nubile body, which was being feverishly caressed by the Count, whose hands were running across her swelling young breasts whilst he tweaked her delicious big nipples between his fingers.

My hand flew to my mouth as I stood silently in the doorway, although, quite frankly, the horny couple were so engrossed in their kissing and cuddling that they did not look up at my arrival and I believe they would have been oblivious if a dozen officers of the Republican Guard had burst into the room! After regaining my composure, I was about to clear my throat noisily so that Yvette and the Count would know of my presence, when it occurred to me as I watched Yvette slide her fingers around the Count's cock, that they would hardly welcome an interruption – and in any case, I was rather enjoying the sight of this erotic show which was unfolding just a few feet away!

So I stayed silent and leaned against the wall as Yvette squeezed Count Gewirtz's sizeable tool with its enormous uncapped purple helmet, which stood bolt upright in her grasp. 'Your Excellency' she observed, 'I know that you must be tired, so why don't you lie down and relax while I ride on your cock?'

'How very thoughtful of you, Yvette,' remarked the Count, taking up her suggestion. And the gorgeous girl licked her lips, climbed on to his lap and slipped her knees along his thighs. Then she put one arm around his neck and felt for his rigid rod with the other, adjusting her position with a sensuous wiggle as she slipped his throbbing chopper between her thighs and into her cunney. When she was satisfied that she had fitted every inch of the Count's cock snugly inside her tingling pussey, she leaned forward so that his shaft was tickling her clitty and whispered, 'Ahh, that's so nice, my cunney simply adores to be filled with a lovely thick prick. Now push up with your hips as I press down, don't worry, even your big chopper won't hurt me!'

She started to work her hips up and down, riding firmly but at a steady, even pace on the veiny shaft of Count Gewirtz's cock, letting it sink all the way into her engorged hirsute crack and holding it there until it was completely engulfed and their pubic hairs were matted together.

Rupert, I do realise that some men feel uncomfortable with this mode of fucking, on the grounds that it places the female in a so-called 'superior' position, but obviously the Count did not subscribe to such foolishness, for he was certainly more than happy to let Yvette's cunt squelch to and fro on his mighty truncheon. Indeed, the Galician nobleman was so taken with this lascivious girl that I saw his body tremble as he announced that he could feel the spunk boiling up in

143

his balls. Yvette ground her bottom down and then began to bounce up and down on his glistening shaft and the Count's body began to jerk upwards in a series of shivering shudders. Yvette must have felt the first arc of jism splash against the walls of her love tunnel, for she screamed out, 'I'm cumming too, Your Excellency, keep shooting your seed, you lovely fucker, a-h-r-e, a-h-r-e, there I go, oh Mon Dieu, what a magnificent spend!'

Almost unknowingly, I had sat down on a chair and slid my hand under my dress to rub my own moistening pussey whilst I watched this enthralling coupling, but when Yvette cried out 'Mon Dieu' it occurred to me that, except for the aforesaid two words, the lusty pair had been speaking to each other in English.

Now why should this be? I asked myself, but even before I could begin to answer my own question, Yvette – who was still speared upon the Count's twitching todger – turned languidly round to me, and said with a husky laugh, 'Well, Diana, did you enjoy the performance?'

Yes, my dear, I immediately realised that the naughty pair had known I had been watching them from the moment I had opened the door, but had nevertheless decided to carry on fucking regardless of the fact! At first, I was slightly cross, to think that I had been foiled by the randy rascals, but then I giggled and said, 'Very much, thank you, Yvette. Indeed, far more than any play I have seen on the stage either here in Paris or in the West End of London.'

Count Gewirtz eased Yvette off his shrunken shaft which flopped sadly on to his thigh and slid his hand down into the crisp thatch of brown curls which decorated her cunt. 'Stop it, Your Excellency,' she murmured halfheartedly. 'What will Diana think of us?'

For reply, I rose from my chair and began to unfasten the hooks on my dress and observed: 'Diana thinks she would very much like to join in!' They laughed as I kicked off my shoes, and before very long I was also rolling around the bed in the nude as we enjoyed a threeway kiss, and I wondered how this ménage à trois might develop.

This was answered for me by the Count who whispered in my ear, 'Diana, I have a fancy to see you play with Yvette's squishy wet pussey.' Well, I had no objection and I looked questioningly at the enchanting French girl, who shrugged her shoulders and said, 'Why not? I adore being sucked by men or women – it makes no difference, as long as they have clever tongues.' She stretched herself out on her back and her hands jiggled with her breasts in the most inviting manner whilst Count Gerwirtz heaved himself up and sat at the foot of the bed, to allow me room to lie down beside the delectable girl.

Without delay, I leaned over and kissed her elongated crimson titties, twirling my tongue around the large rubbery protuberances and flicking them up into a fine state of erection. Then I let my lips travel slowly along her soft creamy white skin down to the damp tangle of hair in the mound of her crotch. I slid my hands round her body to clutch Yvette's firm yet chubby bum cheeks as my own nipples, now hard with desire, rubbed against hers and my mouth moved inexorably towards the pouting lips of her pussey. Instinctively, the sweet creature opened her thighs to make her cunney more accessible to me and I paused for a moment to inhale her musky cuntal aroma, and she purred with pleasure as I licked the wet, swollen lips of her pussey which were aching to be parted by my questing tongue. Lovingly, I licked along her crack and then she gasped when I forced my lips inside her slit and probed inside her juicy quim until I found the hard little bud of her clitty.

'Yes, eat me out,' Yvette breathed sensuously as I rolled her clitty between my lips, sucking furiously upon the juicy sweetmeat till she screamed in delight, wriggling and writhing from side to side, and it was with great difficulty that I was able to stay with the lusty girl as she rubbed herself off against my mouth.

Now as I lapped up her love juice, I felt the mattress bounce as Count Gerwirtz knelt behind me, and I raised my backside high into the air, opening my legs a little so that he could guide his knob into my cunt from behind and fuck me 'doggie-style'. Alas, the sight of a pretty girl being pleasured by another female proved too exciting for him and all the Count succeeded in doing was shooting his seed all over my bum whilst Yvette continued to pour out her pungent libation over my tongue.

Candidly, I was feeling slightly disappointed when I lifted my head from between Yvette's thighs, and turned round to face the Count, but I had not realised how near to the edge of the mattress I was, and I slipped slowly if not ungracefully down on to the rug at the side of the bed.

Count Gewirtz promptly slid down to join me. 'My dear Diana, I know you haven't yet achieved a spend and I'm sad to say that these days another cockstand is out of the question. However, if you will forgive the immodesty, I would be delighted to show you why women all over the world know me as "the gobbling Galician".'

'I would like nothing better,' I replied, and with a nimbleness that belied his years, the Count hauled himself between my legs and immediately buried his face in my crotch, nuzzling his lips against my pussey and then as my legs opened wider, he brought up his head and slipped his forefinger into my seething quim, twisting and turning it inside my cunt until I felt as if an electric current was crackling through my cunney.

My buttocks tensed as he now plunged two and then three fingers in and out of my juicy love box, and every now and then he toyed with my stiff, pulsing clitty. Oh, it was such blissful agony! Somehow, the clever Count knew when I was on the verge of spending, and would suddenly withdraw his fingers and so hold back the tide of approaching orgasm which threatened to burst over me. In the end, though, I cried out that I wanted to cum and I welcomed the release when the 'gobbling Galician' swirled his tongue around my clitty whilst he finger-fucked me to a delicious climax, and I panted with delight as my love juice jetted down over the Count's clever fingers and my saturated clitty sent divine shudders of ecstasy all over my body as I scaled the highest peaks of pleasure.

I lay back with a seraphic smile, but a worried frown now appeared on Count Gewirtz's face as a bead of milky seed flopped down from his tip. 'Oh dear, I'm afraid we must have stained the rug with jism,' he said gloomily. 'I just pray that my cleaners can remove the marks, for the rug is of a rare seventeenth century Turkish design woven only in a small town near the

147

Turkish border and thus extremely valuable. To the best of my knowledge, few examples can be found in Western Europe outside the state museums.'

'Spunk stains can be the very devil,' I agreed as the Count peered closely at the colourfully elegant fabric. 'But a dab of Professor Perrick's Special Spot Remover should remove all traces of our bodily fluids. It has never failed me yet, and I recall one eventful fuck during a country house weekend with Rupert Mountjoy, Dame Hilary Norman and a titled gentleman whose name I must not mention, when we had to clean the walls as well as the carpet, and one application of this excellent product was all that was needed to do the job most thoroughly.'

Rupert, here I must close this hurried letter, but Count Gewirtz would be most grateful if you would send him a small bottle of Professor Perrick's cleansing foam, for it is not available in Paris. His address is 49 Rue de la Paix and naturally he insists on refunding the cost of the purchase and the postage. I leave this task in your capable hands.

Heaps of love and give your randy old cock a rub tonight on my behalf, if, as I hope, you are no longer sharing your bed with a maid-servant.
Diana

I folded the letter and put it back into my pocket and then mopped my brows as I looked down at the tenting bulge between my legs, for reading Diana's epistle had sent my shaft shooting upwards as soon as she had started to describe the saucy goings-on at Count Gewirtz's party. Indeed, I rather fancied going upstairs to relieve my feelings by taking myself in hand, but then I recalled Fred Nolan's reminder about the advice I had been given by Doctor Letchmore – to take an occasional rest from fucking. Hard as it might be to put into practice, he had insisted that a short spell of total abstinence was required to recharge my batteries. So I hauled myself out of my chair and, although my stiff prick was still outlined as it pushed against the confines of my trousers, I walked out into the hall to telephone my Aunt Agatha and offer my apologies for bowing out of her dinner party – and for some peculiar reason, it refused to deflate, even whilst the telephone operator was connecting me with my aunt, and in consequence I was forced to stand facing the wall whilst the butler brought Aunt Agatha to the telephone.

Alas, she was distinctly annoyed when I passed on the news that I would be unable to dine with her on Friday week. 'Rupert, this is most inconvenient – your absence will put my table completely out,' she said irritably. 'Your uncle may now have to dine upstairs, though fortunately he is accustomed to that.'

'My apologies, Aunt Agatha, but I thought you might care to ask cousin Beresford to take my place,' I suggested brightly.

'His name is already on the guest-list,' she replied frostily. 'It was my intention that you and Beresford would sit with Cecily and Gwendolen, the twin daughters of Lady Bracknell. Well, I shall have to try and find a suitable replacement as soon as possible. Goodbye, Rupert.'

'Goodbye, Aunt,' I said, frowning as I replaced the receiver, for, like all gay blades in London, I would have welcomed the opportunity of an introduction to the beautiful Bracknell twins. According to clubland gossip, the girls liked nothing better than to pleasure a man together, with one twin sucking him off whilst he played with the titties and pussey of her sister, or having one twin ride upon the lucky lover's stiffstander whilst the other sat on his face to have her cunney licked out. Naturally, these lewd thoughts did nothing to ease the condition of my aching prick, which was still as stiff as a poker.

'It's all a question of mind over matter,' I muttered to myself, and decided to go downstairs to the kitchen and tell Mrs Riley how much I appreciated her culinary skills, and to hear her suggestions for the menu to be prepared on Monday evening when my new friends Claudia Renouvin and Kitty Forrest were coming to dine with me at Bedford Square.

All was quiet in the servants quarters, although I could hear the sounds of movement from behind the kitchen door. And as I grasped the handle I gave a small grunt of satisfaction, for surely an amiable chat with Mrs Riley would help to convince my cock that it was high time to go to sleep!

But in the famous words of Rabbie Burns: 'the best laid schemes o' mice an' men gang aft a-gley.' It must have been impossible to judge who was more shocked, myself or the new cook, when I flung open the kitchen door to find Mrs

Riley sitting on a chair dressed only in a tight-fitting corset, over the top of which her creamy ripe bosoms overflowed. Yet though her stays were still in place, her knickers were lying at her feet, and in her hands she was holding a black china dildo which was stuffed into the dark hairy thatch between her thighs.

'Pardon me, I'm so sorry to interrupt you,' I gasped, and the buxom cook looked up and gave a little scream when she saw me standing in front of her. Somehow I found the strength to tear my gaze away from her pussey as she jerked the dildo out of her cunt and, with a reddening face, bent down and pulled up her knickers, before answering, 'Oh no, sir, it's entirely my fault. I thought I had locked the kitchen door.'

'Well, we all make mistakes, and be assured that as far as I am concerned there's no great harm done,' I said, determined to put the agitated lady at her ease, as the last thing I wanted was for her to think she must give in her notice. Mrs Riley was a first-class cook and, again, to quote a literary muse [*George Meredith – Editor*]: 'Kissing don't last: cookery do!'

I went on, 'You had no reason to suppose that I might come downstairs. In fact, the purpose of my visit was to congratulate you on the excellent meals you have served since you began work here, and also to ask your advice about Monday night, when two ladies are coming to dine with me.'

To my relief, these words appeared to calm her down and when I suggested that we discussed these matters over a cup of tea, she filled the electric kettle I had been given as a Christmas gift by Madame Marussia of Samarkand [*for a graphic account of Rupert's carnal relations with this uninhibited lady and a number of fun-loving friends, see* An Edwardian Dandy III: Art For Art's Sake – *Editor*].

'I'm glad to see that you are not afraid to use the new kettle,' I remarked approvingly, sitting down at the well-scrubbed wooden table. 'Your predecessor was scared stiff of electricity and insisted on boiling water in the traditional fashion, using the gas cooker.'

'Ah well, some people always prefer the old ways,' she said, switching on the new kettle. 'There are quite a number who still distrust refrigerators and put food in the larder instead. My late husband, Herbert, was like that, although, in his case, it wasn't because he didn't trust refrigerators, he just didn't want to spend good drinking money on something for the house!'

'Oh, I didn't know that you were a widow, Mrs Riley,' I said politely. 'How very distressing it must be to lose a husband so early in life.'

'Not in my case, sir,' she said, setting down cups and saucers on the table. 'Herbert was a policeman whom I met when I started work in my first position at Lord and Lady Brampton's in Belgrave Square and Sussex, after gaining my diploma at Mrs Bickler's School of Domestic Science [*the Edwardian equivalent of the Good Housekeeping Institute – Editor*]. We courted for six months and although I knew that he liked a drink or two, he was very good at, er, you know what. In the end, we got married and I left service to set up house with Herbert in West Hampstead.

'Now as you probably know, sir, a policeman's pay doesn't go very far, but I found myself a job serving in a greengrocer's shop only a few doors away from where we lived, so I couldn't understand why we were always skint. Then Herbert started to come home slightly worse for wear, but he told me it was only because local pubs would insist that he had a drink to keep him going in the cold weather.

'Well, things went from bad to worse, and one morning I found a letter from his chief inspector, warning Herbert that he was liable to be chucked off the force if he didn't cut down on the boozing. When I confronted him with it that evening, he got all uppity and rushed out of the house in a great rage, without even taking off his uniform. He didn't come back home that night, and in the morning, just as I was leaving to go to the station to see if he had spent the night there, there was a knock on the door and two bobbies were on the doorstep to tell me that Herbert had been found unconscious in West End Lane and had been rushed to hospital in an ambulance.'

This interesting anecdote was beginning to sound like one of those short story mysteries in the weekly magazines, and I tried to think what might have happened to the late Mr Riley whilst his widow spooned a generous measure of the Army and Navy's Best Household Blend into the teapot and added boiling water.

'Dear me, what a shocking story,' I commented, as she took a milk jug out of the refrigerator. 'So had Herbert disturbed a gang of thieves who attacked him and left him lying senseless in the street?'

To my surprise, Mrs Riley guffawed and shook her head. 'No, nothing like that! The plain truth was that Herbert had spent the whole evening inside The Cross Keys, and was seen staggering out blind drunk at about eleven o'clock. Unluckily for him, the road is very badly lit near the pub, and he hadn't gone very far when he slipped on a pile of horse dung. Herbert must have been so blotto that he couldn't get himself up, so he went to sleep in the street. Anyhow, when an early morning motor-bus trundled by at about five in the morning, the driver didn't see Herbert and ran over him. They did their best for him in the hospital, but he kicked the bucket a few days later.'

'Poor chap, what a way to go – slipping in a pile of horse-shit,' I commented, but Mrs Riley answered roundly, 'Well, at least he was too pissed to have smelled it! Don't you feel sorry for Herbert, Mr Mountjoy, he left me with so many debts that I had to sell up and go into service again.'

She poured out the tea and commented that the only thing she missed about Herbert was 'a nice bit of slap and tickle in the bedroom', although the drink had adversely affected Herbert's performance during the last months of their

154

marriage. Seemingly oblivious that she was still standing in her underwear, Mrs Riley went on, 'And that's why you found me using this ladies' comforter, which I bought from a surgical store off the Charing Cross Road. It doesn't give the thrill of the genuine article, but it relieves the tension whenever I get the urge to be poked.'

I picked up the prick-shaped artefact and, examining it closely, noticed that it was not after all black, but in fact was painted a very dark blue with a cluster of six small silver stars on the uncapped knob – a design which struck me as somehow familiar. Indeed, I was about to comment upon this when I suddenly recalled where I had seen the pattern before – on the shirt of the jockey riding home a winner at Newmarket – the colours of none other than the lusty baronet Sir Loring Sayers, with whom Beresford and I had recently enjoyed such a grand fuck with Becky and Dora at the Jim Jam Club.

'There isn't anything wrong with it, is there, Mr Mountjoy?' asked Mrs Riley anxiously as I continued to study her dildo carefully. 'I paid eighteen and six [*92p – Editor*] for it at Professor Baum's shop in Dyott Street.'

'No, no, not at all,' I quickly replied, passing the artificial glazed china cock back to her. 'I just find it surprising to see that it is painted in the racing colours of an old acquaintance of mine.'

'You shouldn't really be surprised, sir.' She shrugged. 'Many officers from the Armed Services employ Professor Baum to manufacture dildoes modelled from plaster casts of their own pricks, to give to their wives or lady friends when they are called away on duty.'

I digested this fascinating news with interest, although, to the best of my knowledge, Sir Loring had never donned any military uniform. Mrs Riley must have guessed what was going through my mind for she added, 'Of course, it's also not unknown for some young scamps also to give them to their girl friends as a keepsake at the end of an affair. In these cases, though, there is always the danger that a scorned lover might sell the dildo back to Professor Baum. Let's face it, none of his customers can tell whether they have purchased second-hand articles. It seems that I've done so myself, although it hardly matters so long as it gives satisfaction.'

We drank our tea in silence and then Mrs Riley sighed heavily and said, 'But as I said a few moments ago, there isn't a dildo which can beat the real thing.' She stood up and fiddled with her whalebone corset, then added, 'I must get dressed, sir. This corset is rather uncomfortable . . . could I possibly ask you to help me take it off?'

'Of course you may,' I answered, for I had no objection to playing the lady's maid.

So she stood up and presented her back to me and, after some initial fumbling, I managed to unfasten the garment. However, as it fell to the floor with a resounding thud, Mrs Riley swivelled round, quite naked except for a pair of tight cotton briefs. She stroked her full, globular breasts, caressing her lush tawney titties until they stood up like erect little red-coated

156

Guardsmen in her hands.

'Oh, I'm sorry, Mr Mountjoy, I know I shouldn't say this, but I'd be ever so grateful if you would fuck me. I haven't had a prick in my pussey since I arrived here and I'm simply dying for a good, no-nonsense poke. Feel my juicy red berries – they've been swollen ever since you came in the room and I saw that big bulge between your legs.'

Mrs Riley took hold of my hands and placed them firmly on her enormous rounded bosoms. My fingers closed round her cheekily protruding nipples, which hardened perceptibly under my touch. At the same time, she reached down and gently squeezed my shaft which rapidly thickened up and again threatened to burst out of my trousers – although it was soon released into her hand, and she ripped off two buttons in her haste to undo my fly. She tugged down my trousers and drawers to my ankles and I stepped out of them as our lips met in a hot passionate kiss.

My other clothes soon followed these garments on to the floor as, clutching my stiff cock in a vice-like grip, Mrs Riley sat down on a chair and dragged me over her, rubbing my rigid rod in the valley between her huge bare breasts. And I confess that this novel method of wanking was so exciting that I shot my load there and then. She directed the flow of sticky white jism from my twitching tool over her titties, soaking them with my copious libation. Then she asked me to rub my spunk all over her raised-up nips, a task I found most enjoyable when I felt the erect rubbery titties push up against my fingers.

Now I have always subscribed to the maxim that it is a foolish chap who fucks his domestic staff, as such a course will almost inevitably end with a quarrel and the girl concerned flouncing out of the house when it is made clear to her that she is no longer welcome to share her master's bed. However, in this case, if I didn't fuck Mrs Riley I would probably lose one of the best cooks in London, so I put my principles to one side and let the sensual cook stand up whilst I sat down in the chair. There was little doubt that she desperately wanted to be fucked, because in an instant her tousled dark tresses were lodged between my thighs and she began to coax my semi-erect shaft to swell back up to its former thick throbbing stiffness, moving her clenched fist up and down my hot, quivering cock.

She looked up and with a lively glint in her eyes she said longingly, 'Oooh, what a lovely thick shaft, Mr Mountjoy. It looks nicer than any meaty sausage I've made in this kitchen.' She planted a swift series of butterfly kisses all around my helmet, and then opened her lips wide to encircle my uncapped knob. I let out a gasp of sheer ecstasy as the eager cook swirled her wet tongue all over my smooth domed bell-end.

'Ahhh!' I gurgled as she took my shaft in her hand and worked her fingers up and down, frigging me in rhythm with her bobbing head as she sucked lustily away on my engorged prick.

Again we changed positions, and I pulled up a

footstool, so that Mrs Riley could lie in the seat of the wide old armchair with her legs resting on the stool. Then I adjusted the cushion so that her thickly thatched cunney was positioned at an excellent angle for my bursting cock, which I held in my hand as I moved between her legs, nudging her knees a little further apart as she now took hold of my truncheon and piloted my prick through her buttery bush and into her dripping slit. As she did so, I growled with delight as her cunney muscles nipped the sides of my shaft, and moved my hands towards her colossal bosoms, rubbing my palms against her rubbery titties.

'Oh, thank you, thank you, thank you!' she gabbled as I started to slide my shaft in and out of her yearning quim in a steady rhythm. She purred with delight, relishing the feel of my veiny tool easing back and forth along her love tunnel. I pumped away at a faster pace and the ardent lady arched her body upwards to ensure that every inch of my pulsating prick was embedded inside her juicy cunt. I continued to fuck her until she panted, 'Oh, sir, that's absolutely wonderful, I've come twice already! Now fuck the arse off me, you lovely man!'

I was more than happy to oblige, and increased the tempo until I was sluicing my shaft in and out of her squelchy pussey at top speed. I could hear my balls slap against the back of her thighs as she gripped me round the waist with her legs. In turn, with each forward thrust, I now pinched her elongated strawberry nipples between my thumbs and forefingers until at last I discharged a fountain of frothy spunk in an explosive spend, and her face shone with joy as delicious waves of blissful ecstasy radiated out all over her body from her saturated cunt.

'Oooh, what a gorgeous fuck! Honestly, sir, I haven't been reamed out so thoroughly since Count Gewirtz fucked me last year, when he came over to London for the Berkeley Square Ball. You're every bit as good at fucking as Mary Tothill told me.'

'Mary Tothill?' I said questioningly, and she smiled and went on, 'Surely you must remember Mary? A pretty girl with long dark hair who used to work here as a chambermaid, till she left last summer to take up service with Lord and Lady Brampton, which is where I met her.'

I chuckled as I replied, 'Oh, *that* Mary! Of course I remember her. As you say, she's a very pretty girl. Give her my best wishes, if you keep in touch with one another.'

She nodded and said, 'I will indeed, sir. Mary and I are having tea together on my next half-holiday. Well, Mary told me that she adored being fucked by your lovely big cock, and her present boy friend can't satisfy her pussey like you could.'

'Hmm, how very kind of her to say so,' I observed with mixed feelings; for whilst I was hardly displeased to hear such a fulsome compliment on my abilities between the sheets, I was hardly enthralled at the idea that my prick might be a subject for discussion below-stairs at the Brampton's town house in Belgrave Square.

But Mrs Riley must have seen that her remark had caused me some concern, for she hurriedly continued, 'Please don't worry, Mr Mountjoy. Mary was never one to gossip with the other servants about her love life. In fact, she never mentioned anything about any high jinks here until I told her I was coming to work for you.'

'That's good to hear,' I said with great relief. 'Because I wouldn't ever be able to look young Philippa, Lord Brampton's daughter, in the eye again if I thought she knew all the lurid details of my private life.' To my surprise, these words caused the cook to burst out into peals of hearty laughter and I asked her what was so amusing.

'Oh dear, I shouldn't really have laughed,' she said, wiping her eyes with the backs of her hands. 'It was just the idea of Miss Philippa being shocked by any rude tale!'

'What on earth do you mean?' I said rather stiffly, picking up my spun silk pants from the floor. 'Philippa Brampton is a very attractive girl who has only recently returned home after attending a finishing school in Switzerland. I would have imagined that she was totally inexperienced in relations with the opposite sex.'

She looked at me in astonishment and cried out, 'Philippa Brampton inexperienced? You must be joking, Mr Mountjoy! Why, that girl has had more pricks up her crack than I've had hot dinners!'

Now it was my turn to be amazed, for this sweet seventeen-year-old daughter of the Bramptons – one of the wealthiest old Sussex landowning families – gave the impression of knowing nothing of the ways of the world. I told Mrs Riley how my cousin Beresford had once declared, that he believed Philippa Brampton would blush if a word like 'trousers' or 'legs' came up in conversation.

'Well, it's not my place to say anything, but I can't believe that we're talking about the same girl,' opined Mrs Riley, standing up and slipping her knickers on.

Whilst we dressed ourselves (and after I had promised that her remarks would be treated in the strictest confidence), Mrs Riley told me a tale about Philippa Brampton that I found absolutely astounding and which, not for the first time, showed me how true is the old saying that one must never judge a book by its cover.

She began by saying how Miss Philippa had asked to be taught some basic culinary skills and how the two of them had become quite friendly. Then she went on, 'Miss Philippa liked nothing better than to wander into my room for a cup of tea and a chat,' she reminisced, buttoning up her dress. 'And more often than not she would tell me all about her latest beau – and she wasn't backward in coming forward with the lurid details about the boy concerned, from the colour of the hairs on his chest to the length of his todger, if you'll pardon the expression.'

She frowned and then said reflectively, 'Mind you, when I come to think of it, I can see why you were so surprised when I said that she liked nothing better than a bit of slap and tickle. She never mentioned anything about having an affair with any gentlemen, but always told me about some lusty pokes she had enjoyed with a lad from the village after she had come back to town from a long weekend down in the country at Brampton Lodge.

'The last fuck I remember Miss Philippa telling me about was with a boy named Alexander Woodside, the sixteen-year-old son of the local vicar. It happened during a warm afternoon early last September, when she had gone out for a walk after luncheon.

'She said to me: "It was such a gorgeously warm day and golden shafts of light were coming from the sun which was shining almost overhead, so that my eyes were half closed whilst I was walking through the lush long grass in one of Farmer Harrison's meadows. And I accidentally tripped over Alexander Woodwise, who was lying on his back on a convenient hummock of earth, and so wrapped up in reading the book he held, that he had not heard me approach. I sprawled over him and the book went flying from his hands. 'Oh, I beg your pardon, Alex, I should have been looking where I was going,' I said, scrambling to my knees and reaching out to pass his book back to him. He seemed a little agitated, although he said, 'That's all right, Miss Philippa, no harm done. May I have my book back, please?'

' " 'Certainly you may,' I said, and was about to hand it back to him when I noticed the title on the spine of the volume – the young scamp had been reading a bound copy of *The Oyster* for 1899! 'Here you are, Alex, although I don't believe that your father would approve you reading a saucy book like that. Did somebody give this book to you?'

' "His cheeks reddened and he muttered, 'One of the chaps at school lent it to me, though of course I've hidden it from my father.'

' "I looked down at this good-looking boy, almost eighteen months younger than me, but strongly built and tall for his age. 'Well, don't worry, I shan't tell him. At sixteen, you're quite old enough to read gallant literature if you want to,' I said. And then I saw that the outline of a very interesting bulge had formed in his trousers. So I moved my hand lazily across his thigh and ran my palm against the outline of his stiffie. 'Why, Alex, reading ribald stories from *The Oyster* has obviously excited you – but I don't suppose you've ever had the chance to do more than read about the joys of *l'art de faire l'amour*.'

' "The dear boy blushed furiously as he confessed that he had never had the opportunity to do more than kiss a girl whilst playing Postman's Knock at his female cousin's birthday parties. Now, the idea that this handsome boy was still a virgin whetted my appetite and, licking my lips, I pulled open the buttons of Alex's fly and, slipping my hand inside the slit of his drawers, I brought out his pulsing smooth shaft into the sunlight. I gasped at the size of his bare cock, for it must have been at least eight inches long and was one of the thickest I had ever seen. It bucked and bounded in my hand, bursting with youthful vigour, and instantly I knew I had to have it in my mouth there and then.

' "I don't think he realised what I had in mind when I knelt there before him and took hold of that fine youthful cock and licked around the purple helmet. He audibly panted out his delight: 'Oh, that feels so amazingly nice, Miss Philippa,' he gasped, and I said with a smile 'It feels very nice for me as well, Alex, knowing that I am the very first girl to suck your lovely prick.'

' "I brought my lips down and let my tongue run the full length of his shaft, running back to the knob to lick up a sticky drop of pre-cum which had formed on his knob. Then I opened my mouth and gulped in at least four inches of his hot cock into my mouth, then closed my lips around this enormous fleshy lollipop and moved my tongue across its width. I sucked greedily, and naturally he spent almost immediately, shooting jets of creamy spunk down my throat. I would have liked to have continued with a proper fuck, but we heard the sound of voices approaching from the nearby wood, so he hastily pushed his still stiff wet cock back into his trousers and I scrambled to my feet. We never had a chance to be alone together again, but there's bound to be an opportunity to fuck the sweet boy in the future." '

The cook smacked her lips and gave me a vulpine smile as she concluded, 'There you are, sir, that is as near enough a word-for-word account of how Miss Philippa sucked off the vicar's son, and I promise you I haven't embroidered or changed anything that she told me.'

'Well, I'm very grateful to you,' I said slowly and tugged at my groin where my shaft was back at bursting point after hearing this randy if second-hand story of Philippa Brampton's secret love life. This made me remember that I had hardly followed my physician's advice to ease up on my carnal activities, so I quickly changed the subject and said, 'Do you know something, Mrs Riley, for some reason I'm feeling quite peckish again, even after your delicious luncheon.'

She gave a hoarse chuckle and said, 'So am I, sir. It's the fucking that does it, you know. I always say that you need a slap-up feed after a poke. Shall I prepare a nice salad with some cold roast beef for tea?'

'A jolly good idea, Mrs Riley, that would be splendid, but in that case, please don't put out any bread and butter, sandwiches, or tea-cake, for there's no doubt that I need to lose some weight,' I replied, giving my belly a light pat. I was convinced that I was at least half a stone heavier since the turn of the year, and lately had been avoiding standing on the bathroom weighing machine after my morning shower.

She shook her head and said, 'Come now, Mr Mountjoy, a fine, well-built young man like you doesn't have to diet.' Then she winked at me and added, 'If you want to take more exercise, though, a police surgeon once told me that a first-class fuck is the equivalent of a three-mile walk, and I'm always ready for a long hike!'

'I'll remember that,' I said hastily, and slipped on my jacket and beat a hasty retreat from the randy cook before any of the servants spotted me there. I hurried out and, taking the steps two at a time, dashed all the way up the stairs to the billiards room on the second floor, where I had fixed up the door hooks for use with my Whitely Exerciser [*'home gymnastics' apparatus and 'obesity removers' were extremely popular amongst the Edwardian upper classes – hardly surprising when one considers the enormous meals they tucked away – Editor*]. I took off my jacket and, gripping hold of the handles, raised my arms high above my head and pulled on the elastic cables. For fifteen minutes I performed the body, arm and leg exercises, and would have continued had there not been a knock on the door and Selina, the pretty little blue-eyed parlourmaid whom I had occasionally let into my mind when lack of a genuine pussey had forced me to indulge in satisfying Mr Pego's needs by a meeting with Madame Thumb and her Four Daughters, came into the room.

'I'm sorry to interrupt you, sir, but Mr Beresford is hanging on the telephone for you,' said the girl rather nervously, but she giggled when I dropped the straps of the exerciser and said, 'Is he now, Selina – well, is he standing or sitting on it? Tell my cousin he can get off it as soon as he likes – either way, it must be awfully uncomfortable for him!' Then I mopped my brow and followed her downstairs.

'Berry, are you there? Sorry to have kept you waiting, old chap. What can I do for you?'

'Hello, Rupert, I'm sorry to trouble you, but I've just closed the front door on Aunt Agatha,' he said grimly. 'She called round unexpectedly this afternoon, and gave me a stern lecture on what calamities would rain down on me if I didn't make an appearance at her blessed dinner party on Friday week, especially after you had dropped out at the last minute.'

'Hardly the last minute! I called her earlier today, and the party isn't till late next week!' I said with some indignation. 'Anyhow, don't you remember that just before we fucked those two jolly girls at the Jim Jam Club, I said to you that I had been invited to join a party going to Aintree to watch the Grand National?'

'Yes, but you've obviously forgotten that I told you that I was also going up to see the race, with Sir Loring Sayers' crowd from the Club!' he snapped back sharply. 'I only received a hand-delivered invitation this morning, so thanks to you putting forward my name as your substitute, I'm really in the soup.'

'I didn't do any such thing,' I replied warmly. 'As I just informed you, I only spoke to Aunt Agatha a couple of hours ago, well after you received your invitation. To be frank, I did ask her to invite you in my place, but she said that your name was already on the guest list. She was rather cross when I said I couldn't make it, so it appears that someone else must have also let her down.'

'Oh, well, in that case I suppose you can't be blamed,' grunted Beresford with a sigh. 'But it's a damned shame, because I was really looking forward to travelling up to the races with Sir Loring – although I'm so stony broke that I would have had to ask you for a small loan to help me out till the old man's cheque comes in at the end of next month. In fact, I dare not offend Aunt Agatha, because one word from her to my father would be enough for him to cancel my allowance. He's been on at me for months to come back home and help run the family estate.'

The thought went through my head that there, but for the grace of Uncle Humphrey and his friend Colonel Wright, go I. Now I sympathised with my cousin, saying, 'Bad luck, old boy. But if Aunt Agatha has not already told you, it may be some consolation for you to know that the delectable Bracknell twins will be sitting on either side of you at Aunt Agatha's table.'

This news immediately brightened Beresford up, and he said with a fresh tone of excitement in his voice, 'The Bracknell twins! Rupert, are you sure? Both the celestial Cecily and the glamorous Gwendolen? Yes, indeed, that is a great comfort. Why, I would have thought that you would have been tempted to cancel your own trip to sit next to those gorgeous girls!'

'I shall indeed be sorry to have missed the opportunity of making their acquaintance,' I agreed with a chuckle. 'And, as I am sure that there is at least a grain of truth in the stories about the Bracknell girls, you are certain to enjoy a most stimulating evening.'

Beresford was now in the best of spirits. All the

anger in his voice was gone when he said, 'I'll tell you all the juicy details when you get back home. Oh, by the way, whilst you're at Aintree, could you put a bet on for me? One of the waiters at the Jim Jam told me that he had some inside information that it would be worth staking a fiver on Johnstown Lad. Would you put a tenner each way for me when you make your own bets?'

My head jerked back in horror as I listened to this request. 'A tenner each way? But you were told you should only stake a fiver on the blessed horse!' I was about to remonstrate further with my cousin when he cut in and said, 'Oh, I know it's a hell of a gamble, Rupert, but the tradesmen will begin to cut off supplies if I don't start paying their bills, and Mr Rabinowitz has threatened to take back my new Norfolk Jacket [*a popular sports jacket, single-breasted and belted with a box-pleat down the back – Editor*] unless I cough up a cheque by next Wednesday, so I'm desperate to rake in a few shekels.'

Now Beresford may have had many choice epithets thrown at him (especially by ladies, during the time he was influenced by his old college friend Freddie Newman, whose idea of wooing was 'treat 'em mean, keep 'em keen' but his hand has always been first to grab a pen and sign the bill after a night with a party of congenial companions at the Jim Jam Club, and I knew that he hated not meeting his household bills every month, especially as far as small shopkeepers were concerned. So I said briskly, 'Look here, old boy, if things are that bad, don't throw good money away on the gee-gees. You can always borrow a few quid from me if times are tough. For a start, I have to see Mr Rabinowitz next Tuesday morning for a fitting and whilst I'm there, I'll pay your bill.'

There was a short pause and then he said, 'You're a good egg, Rupert, and I appreciate the offer. All right, I would be grateful if you would settle up with Sam Rabinowitz. He's been very patient even though I've had to keep him waiting for something like five months.'

'Are you sure I can't help out any more?'

'No, but if I find myself sinking deeper in the mire, I won't hesitate to call you. In the meantime, please don't forget to put that wager on Johnstown Lad for me. Oh, hold on a moment, Rupert – must dash – Gerry Gascoigne and Tim Shackleton have just turned up for tea. Look, I'm out of town till Wednesday, so if I don't see you before your trip, *bon voyage* and have a great time.'

He rang off and I grimaced as I replaced the receiver on its hook, for Beresford's request had put me in a dilemma – should I or should I not comply with his request to place this large wager for him? The odds were very much against anyone picking the winner in a race like the Grand National, a steeplechase where even the fastest horses were often impeded or brought down by one of the other runners. If I followed his instructions, the chances were that my cousin would be twenty pounds more in debt, though only to me, of course, and I would hardly make him bankrupt if he couldn't pay back the money.

However, on the other hand, my allowance from Uncle Humphrey was not so high that I could afford to chuck cash willy-nilly into the bookmakers' satchels.

Yet Johnstown Lad was fancied by quite a few newspaper tipsters to have a sporting chance in the big race, and if I didn't put on the bet, and Beresford's choice did win, I might well find myself owing my cousin as much as three hundred pounds! Even if the bloody nag came second or third, I would have to fork out around fifty sovs if I decided to act as Beresford's personal bookie!

What a difficult choice I had to make! Still, I had plenty of time to think what would be the best way to solve the problem, so I resolved to put the matter from my mind and pop upstairs for a little billiards practice before tea. This would help me to forget Beresford's problem and would also keep my thoughts on the straight and narrow, for I needed to take other exercises besides fucking if I were to give of my best to Amber Berlynne at the Adelphi Hotel on the night before the big race.

I was very proud of my new twelve-foot billiards table, which I had purchased for sixty guineas at Messrs Selfridge in their January sale. It was handsomely built on eight solid mahogany legs, with an extra stout best Welsh slate bed, covered in superfine West of England baize cloth, making it fit for play by such luminaries of the sport as His Majesty the King and his lifelong friends Mr Charles Carrington [*with whom King Edward VII enjoyed a robust taste in 'gallant' literature – Editor*] and Mr Christopher Sykes.

So when I opened the door of the billiards room, I was at first astounded and then greatly angered by the sight of Selina, standing stark naked on a footstool, bent over the billiards table, her strong, coltish legs set slightly apart and the shapely cheeks of her firm young bottom being caressed by my footman, Edwards, who was hastily peeling off his trousers. When he had finished, he grasped his erect swollen chopper in his hand and brazenly announced, 'Right, my girl, it's time to brace yourself, because I'm now going to slip my prick up your lovely bum. Hold on a moment, I'm just going to spread some cooking butter on my shaft to help me slide it in without hurting you.' He smeared a liberal amount of butter on his bulging cock and Selina reached behind her and taking hold of his sturdy shaft, directed its ruby knob between the glorious globes of her delicious backside to the puckered little rosette of her rear dimple which winked invitingly at him.

I had been struck speechless by the effrontery of the pair, but the thought that the superb green baize of my table would soon be stained by their love juices jerked me into speech.

'Hey, you two randy jack-rabbits! Get off that table this instant!' I thundered. 'How dare you use this room for your own amusements! If you've marked that table, Edwards, I'll take the cost of repair out of your wages.'

Their heads spun round and Edwards slapped his cheek in horror, gasping, 'Selina, you told me that you had locked the door!'

'No, I said have *you* locked it?' she replied, trying to hide her face in her hands. Before I could draw breath and give them both notice, Edwards regained some of his composure and said, 'Sir, I promise you that there's no need to worry about the condition of your table – look, I've spread a thick absorbent cloth over the baize – there is no way it could be damaged. And I beg of you, Mr Mountjoy, please don't discharge Selina over this business. It was all my idea to come up here. The fact is, I simply couldn't wait till Tuesday night to fuck her.'

'I don't understand you,' I said stiffly.

'Selina and I have been going out for the last month, sir, but we can't find anywhere private to have a little kiss and cuddle.'

You were doing a bit more than having a kiss and cuddle, I thought to myself as Edwards carried on: 'You see, sir, Selina shares a room with Esme, so we can't go there, and the wall between my own room and Mrs Harrow's is so thin that, frankly, neither of us has much real privacy. Now Esme is staying out overnight on Tuesday, because she is taking two days of her holiday to go and see her parents down in Margate, but the notion of knowing that we were going to enjoy a night's love-making next week was so exciting . . .' His voice trailed off and I finished his words for him: 'That you just couldn't wait any longer, hmm?' My footman nodded and hung his head, and I slowly expelled my breath whilst I decided what action I should take in respect of their gross misconduct.

Now I know that most people I know would have dismissed the couple on the spot, but as a fellow cocksman, and looking at the soft creamy bum cheeks of the pretty girl, I could not help but feel a certain sympathy with my manservant who had performed his duties well enough and, when necessary, had always shown discretion concerning my own rather irregular habits since I had moved into the house. Some French chap [*actually Madame Anne Bigot de Cornuel! – Editor*] once wrote something on the lines that 'No man is ever a hero to his valet' but Edwards gave the impression that he genuinely enjoyed working for me, and in any case I hated giving anyone the sack. So I drew myself up to my full height and said, 'Well, in the circumstances, Edwards, I'm prepared to overlook this affair, especially as you had the foresight to bring up a cloth to ensure that there wouldn't be any stains on the baize.

'However, you have behaved very badly and there is no doubt that you are entirely to blame. After all, such carelessness in not locking the door is quite unforgivable. Whilst I accept that any red-blooded man worth his salt would be driven to distraction in finding somewhere to fuck an attractive girl like Selina as soon as possible, you really should have tried harder to find a better location. For heaven's sake, why didn't you have a word with Mrs Riley? She seems a good sort to me, and I'm sure she would have given you the use of her room if you had asked her. Still, you both deserve to be reprimanded and your punishment is that, until you find elsewhere, you will have to postpone your fucking. I need to use the billiards table for its proper purpose and sink a few red balls into the pockets.'

The incongruousness of these ill-chosen words made it difficult for me to prevent a smile from forming on my lips, but I managed to keep a stern expression on my face – with increasing difficulty as I watched Selina's beautiful breasts jiggle enticingly as she moved across to the chair upon which she had laid her clothes. They dressed themselves quickly and as they left, Edwards whispered something in the girl's ear which I did not catch before they shut the door behind them.

I picked up the triangular wooden frame from the hook on the wall, for I was of a mind to practice some shots in preparation for the snooker competition at the Jim Jam Club next Wednesday night. I had just begun to place the red balls inside it when there was a timid knock at the door.

'Come in,' I called out and, to my surprise, the door half opened and Selina wriggled through the gap before shutting it behind her. She came up to me and said shyly, 'Sorry to interrupt you, sir, but Eddie – I mean, Mr Edwards – left the protective cloth on the floor, and he asked me to get it back for him.'

'Very well, Selina, by all means, take it away,' I said, and I twisted the end of my cue inside a knob of French chalk whilst the curvaceous girl dropped to her knees to gather up the cloth which was lying at my feet. I placed my legs apart and bent forward to strike the white ball with my cue when I felt a soft hand sliding up my leg until it reached my groin. I straightened up immediately and gasped, 'Selina, what the blue blazes do you think you're up to?'

Of course this was, to say the least, a rather unnecessary question, especially when the wanton little minx began to rub her palm sinuously against my thickening shaft, whilst with the other hand she started to unbutton my flies.

Nevertheless, she looked up at me with a smile and said, 'Oh, please don't be cross with me, sir. I just want to show my appreciation for your kindness in overlooking what happened in here a few moments ago.'

'Thank you, that's very thoughtful of you, but really there's no need to go as far as this,' I stammered whilst she proceeded to slide her hand into my drawers and bring out my hot stiff prick into view.

'Oh, I say,' I panted. With a knowing smile, Selina grasped my throbbing boner tight and swirled her pink tongue around my uncapped helmet. 'You're playing with fire, you know.' But she chose to disregard my warning and gently squeezed my balls, softly giggling at the way my cock leaped and bounded in her fist.

She moistened her lips and again washed her tongue over the wide dome of my knob, before giving each of my balls a friendly little suck. Then she transferred her attention back to my fiery red knob, lapping around the 'eye' before taking my tool into her mouth, her wet lips straining to encircle it. I moaned with delight when she started to bob her head up and down my pulsating prick until she sucked it deep into her throat, all the way up to my short and curlies.

I closed my eyes as I jerked my hips to and fro, fucking her mouth in long, sweeping strokes whilst she played with my balls, but I was so stimulated by this wonderful palating that in no time at all the sticky white seed was gushing out of my cock, and the sweet girl gulped it down, smacking her lips with undisguised relish.

'What a splendid sucking off, Selina!' I wheezed, leaning back on the side of the billiards table, my chest heaving with the exertion of the delicious climax. 'It all finished too quickly, though, and you must accept my apologies for spending so quickly.'

'No, no, it was my fault,' insisted the delightful young housemaid, brushing back her pretty mop of curls from her face. 'I shouldn't have squeezed your ballsack whilst I was sucking you, it always leads to boys spending almost immediately afterwards.'

'Well, you're an excellent fellatrice, Selina, you must really enjoy taking a cock between your teeth,' I commented as I crammed my cock back into my trousers. And the uninhibited girl nodded in agreement and said, 'Oh yes, sir, I think I prefer it to fucking. I do so love to lick the smooth wide knob and then lap down the underside of the shaft – it always drives the lads wild. I don't mind if they come before I'm ready to spend because I find it so exciting when a boy squirts out his spunky tribute down my throat – and I adore the flavour of cock juice. I can't think of anything else which tastes so fine and clean.'

I helped her to her feet and said, 'Well, jolly good. The best encounters are always when both partners have achieved satisfaction. The only thing that worries me slightly is how Edwards is going to feel if he ever finds out about this?'

'Oh, Eddie won't mind at all, sir,' she answered carelessly. 'Between ourselves, it was his idea that I should give you a gobble.'

'Was it now?' I said, for some reason slightly irritated by this news, until it occured to me that whoever's idea it had been, it would have been foolish to look a gift horse in the mouth, so to speak! So I chuckled and added, 'Well, as I said, Selina, you did a first-class job and you can suck my prick any time you like!'

On that happy note, the housemaid left me to my own devices and after an hour's practice (in which I notched up a break of thirty-seven) I went downstairs and tucked into the roast beef and salad which Mrs Riley had prepared for tea. Then, after a short nap, I read the afternoon paper and changed into a dinner jacket before leaving the house at seven o'clock for supper at the Jim Jam Club, and hopefully a few good rubbers of bridge.

Alas, although the food in the Club dining-room was as good as ever, in the bridge tournament, I had the misfortune to partner one of our foreign guests, Prince Helmut of Hesse, who was keen enough on the game, but was not only a poor player of the cards but a reckless bidder. On one hand he pushed me into such a small slam, and when he put down his hand it was clear that even with the wind in my sails, I had not the slightest chance of making more than nine tricks at best. If Beresford or Andy Coles had made such a preposterous bid, I would have had quite a lot to say, using some choice phrases heard more often from the lips of porters in Billingsgate Fish Market than in the lush surrounds of a West End gentleman's club. However, I could hardly insult a guest, and a royal personage at that, so I merely remarked in a doleful voice, 'All I can say about that hand, Your Highness, is God save the Prince and preserve Mr Rupert Montjoy!'

To his credit, the Prince roared with laughter, and at the end of the evening informed his officer-in-attendance that I was to be awarded the Hessian Order of Valour, Third Class. '*Danke schön*, Your Highness, but I have no military prowess. Why, I have never even fired a gun in anger, let alone fought a duel with swords or pistols.'

'Maybe not, Rupert, but to partner me in bridge is in itself a battle of the nerves, *nein*?' laughed the Prince who, despite my protestations, insisted in paying our considerable losses to our opponents himself.

So, in spite of my chagrin at performing so poorly in the tournament (won incidentally by Lord Cheetham and Sir Trewin Highgate, who each collected an engraved two-handed silver cup on a plinth for their pains), I was in a good enough mood when I returned home at about midnight. The evening finished on a low note, however, for waiting for me on the hall table was a hand-delivered letter from Claudia Renouvin, informing me that due to unforeseen circumstances neither she nor Kitty Forrest would be able to dine with me on Monday night as planned, although if I wished to telephone her, she would gladly try to rearrange our meeting.

This was a pity, but the tone of the note suggested that the girls really did want to see me again and had not simply changed their minds about furthering our acquaintance. I resolved to call Claudia in the morning and was so tired that I did not even open the new edition of *The Oyster*, but switched off the electric light and fell fast asleep the moment my head touched the pillow.

CHAPTER FOUR

Adventures at Aintree

WHEN I TELEPHONED CLAUDIA RENOUVIN the next day, my feeling that her excuse to postpone our dinner date was genuine was sadly confirmed. When the girls had returned from the theatre last night, a telegram from Lord Brettenham in Baden Baden was waiting for Claudia, which stated that her mentor Sir Bernard Barnes had been taken ill and was now in the spa's hospital.

'I shall book a ticket this morning to go out and see poor Bernard,' she said. I urged her not to be impetuous.

'By all means, have a trunk packed, but don't go haring off to Germany just yet. Hopefully, Bernard will soon recover and will be back here in London in a week or so. Why not fire off a telegram asking Lord Brettenham for further details? If this merely means they will return a few days later than expected, there's no earthly reason for you to go out there. And honestly, Claudia, whilst I don't wish to sound callous, if you do discover that poor Bernard is seriously ill,

182

you should call his sister Mrs Stephanie Owen, and inform her of the situation. She lives somewhere in Surrey, and although she is not very close to her brother, your housekeeper should have her address. If not, I will find it out myself from one of Bernard's close friends.'

There was a brief silence at the end of the line and then Claudia said, 'Rupert, you are so kind – and sensible too. Thank you for your advice. I will send Lord Brettenham a telegram straight away.'

'That's the thing, and I'm sure you'll find that old Bernard will be up and about very soon,' I said cheerfully. 'He's probably just drunk too much of those blinking spa waters. I know it's supposed to do wonders for the liver, but from personal experience it's devilishly easy to overdo it, because there's not much else to do there. A chap I know came back from Baden Baden with a nasty chill last year, which took quite some time to shake off.'

'Really?' said Claudia. 'Oh yes,' I said comfortingly, 'but of course he made a full recovery.' I thought it best not to sketch in the details about the Honourable Warwick Bailey, who had contracted this heavy cold in Baden Baden, not from drinking the waters, but from the effects of coupling in the cold night air with Helga, the younger daughter of Frau Blomberg, the owner of the hotel in which he was staying. I concluded by saying, 'Call me again when you hear further news of Bernard. I am in town until early next Friday morning, then I am leaving to attend a major sporting event in the North of England and will not be back until the following Monday or Tuesday.'

'Not the Grand National?' she asked, and when I replied in the affirmative she laughed and said, 'Why, what a coincidence! Kitty has been invited to join a group of people going to see the race, and she will also be taking the train to Liverpool on Friday.'

We soon established that Kitty and I were travelling on the same train and I asked Claudia to tell her friend that I would be delighted if Kitty would like to journey to Liverpool with me.

'I am certain she would welcome such a charming escort,' said Claudia. 'Rupert, I will ask her to call you later today, and I will telephone you as soon as I have further news about Bernard.'

Kitty contacted me later that day and was very pleased to accept my invitation to travel with her up to Liverpool. She had already booked a seat in the first class 'Ladies Only' compartment, but I told her that I would change the booking and would pick her up at her apartment in Belsize Park at nine o'clock sharp on the following Friday morning. Until then, I led a quiet, almost sedentary life, working like a beaver in the library until luncheon, catching up on all my correspondence, including the composition of a long, if bowdlerised newsy letter to my Mama and taking brisk, long constitutional walks in the afternoon.

In order to lose those unwanted pounds off my tummy, I ate only lightly, and to keep myself in

184

trim for Amber, I even eschewed all forms of fucking (though it would have taken a far stronger willed man than I to tell Selina not to gobble my cock when I came out of the bathroom one morning, dressed only in a towelling robe, to find the nubile girl kneeling in front of my bed) and as my strict regimen included an hour's exercise with dumb-bells and a chest expander every night, by the time I crawled into bed, I was too tired even to raise a cockstand, let alone perform with Mrs Riley, who let it be known that she always slept with her door on the latch!

Edwards had ordered a Prestoncrest private car to be at Bedford Square on the day of my departure at half past eight in the morning. We would pick up Kitty Forrest in Belsize Park and journey on to Euston in good time to catch the Liverpool Express. [*Interestingly, Rupert Mountjoy and several other writers of Edwardian 'horn' books make mention of the Prestoncrest Company, which was used by the more raffish elements in Society. The drivers, who were always addressed as 'Graham', regardless of their real names, were not only noted for their punctuality and driving skills, but also for their total discretion, and many Society liaisons were conducted (sometimes actually in the vehicles) with the participants knowing that nothing that was said or done inside a Prestoncrest car would become public knowledge – Editor*]

On the afternoon before I left London, in the nick of time, I received a reply from old Goldhill, the Mountjoy family retainer, with his tip for the big race 'straight from the horse's mouth', so to speak. He wrote:

Dear Mr Rupert,

It's a mug's game trying to win on the Grand National, especially with such a big field, so you would be wise just to have an each-way flutter on a rated outsider and then hope for the best.

Anyway, if I were going to Aintree, I would probably back Mr Whitaker's mount, The Lawyer III, or if you really want to chance your arm, stake a small amount on an American bred horse named Rubio. This gelding won three races in 1903 when for some reason he broke down, but Mr Bletsoe the trainer nursed it back to health by lending it to a friend who owned the Prospect Arms Hotel in Towcester, with the instruction that it should pull the hotel bus to and from the station every day. [This is absolutely true – Editor] I hear that this unusual treatment has worked so well that the horse is back in training and by all accounts is now fighting fit.

Have a good time, sir, and I'd be most grateful if you would put a bob each way on both The Lawyer III and Rubio for me.
Respectfully yours,
Stanley Goldhill

I folded his letter carefully and slipped it into my wallet, then went upstairs to supervise the packing of my trunk, which was on the large size for a short trip, but into which I could pack some extra clothes, should I be able to stay on an extra day or so with the delectable Lady Amber Berlynne.

186

'Don't forget to pack my new dressing-bag,' I said to Edwards as he placed a pile of shirts into the battered portmanteau. I always travel with luggage which has seen better days, a stratagem which has so far saved me from the attention of the gangs of light-fingered gentlemen who frequent the ports and main-line railway stations all over the world.

'Very good, sir,' he replied, dusting some fluff from my slippers before putting them inside my case. 'Are there any items inside it which need to be replaced?'

'No, though as this will be the first time I have used it since Uncle Humphrey gave it to me at Christmas, you may as well check the contents – although he purchased the bag from Harrods, so I would be astonished if anything were found to be missing.'

I sat on the bed whilst Edwards finished his work and said idly, 'It must be a great relief to have a willing and attractive lass like Selina on hand. After all, pretty young girls like her don't grow on trees and in any case, I would imagine that with limited time available to seek pleasures outside the house, it must be somewhat difficult for servants to engage in social intercourse with members of the opposite sex.'

'It can be extremely difficult, sir,' agreed Edwards with a wry smile. 'Although one can be fortunate and find employment with a liberal employer such as yourself. It also helps if the mistress of the house is, ah, shall we say *free* with her favours with selected servants.'

I said with a chuckle, 'Oh, you must be referring to ladies like Mrs Tolscomber and Lady Roddieford, who left their husbands to set up homes with their butlers.'

'Quite so, sir. Although such an opportunity to leave service has never come my way,' he replied solemnly. 'However, when I first entered service as a young seventeen-year-old footman in a large country establishment, I was seduced by the mistress of the house.'

'Were you, by Jove!' I exclaimed in surprise, for whilst many gentlemen regarded the maids as fair game, it was unusual for well-to-do ladies to take their pleasure with male servants. 'Well, don't stop there – tell me all whilst you finish packing. I'm sure the story will be more interesting than anything I'll find in the *Evening News*.'

'By all means, sir, but I would appreciate it if the anecdote is not repeated,' he said respectfully. 'For whilst the lady concerned is now living in Ceylon, I would not want to spread any gossip which might damage her social standing.'

'Very commendable, Edwards. You have my word that anything you say will go no further,' I assured him. 'Carry on, I'm all ears.'

'Well, I should start by saying that without doubt Lady – ah, let's call her Maud – was definitely neglected by her husband. He would go to London and stay at his club for days at a time, leaving his wife to her own devices, which I thought was most unfair since they had only a scattering of friends in the vicinity. I overheard the housekeeper tell the butler that the marriage was rather a sham, made only to join the two family estates which had been going through hard times, and that the master of the house rarely shared the same bed as his wife, but took his pleasures elsewhere. Even if this were true, I found it hard to understand. Lady Maud was a most attractive woman of no more than thirty, and I would have liked nothing better than to be given the chance to give her ladyship satisfaction in the absence of her husband.

'Now Lady Maud was very fond of riding and every morning, come rain or shine, I opened the front door for her, and in the driveway a groom would be standing with her horse, waiting to help her mount for her morning gallop. Well, on one sunny spring day, she also went out riding in the afternoon. When she came back, the groom took away her horse and, still dressed in her tight riding breeches, she strode through into the garden and instructed me to bring her a pot of tea and a plate of digestive biscuits.

'I'll be in the summer-house,' she called, and I carried out her refreshment on a tray to the back of the garden where the summer-house stood near three large elm trees. She had already set up a table upon which I placed the tray, and then she ordered me to bring out blankets and pillows from the summer-house, because she fancied the idea of picnicking on the warm grass. I did as she asked, but whilst I spread the blanket she bent down, deliberately flaunting the taut rounded cheeks of her bottom straining inside the skin-tight beige material of her riding breeches.

'Lady Maud deliberately fiddled around for a few moments, plumping up the pillows, until she suddenly straightened up and, looking directly at the bulge in the front of my trousers, said in an amused tone of voice; "Edwards, I do believe that you have been staring at my backside. What have you to say? You may tell me the truth, there is no need to be shy." Of course, I was speechless by her frankness and my face reddened as she went on: "I'm very flattered that a seventeen-year-old lad like you should get a cockstand from looking at my arse. Come closer and put your hand all round and under it and tell me what it feels like."

' "It's really lovely, ma'am. May I keep my hand there?" I croaked, and she laughed out loud and answered: "Yes, of course you may, dear boy. And if you slide your fingers through the cleft you will find my cunney, which would like nothing better than to have your strong young cock sliding inside it."

' "Do you really want me to fuck you, Lady Maud?" I gasped with bashful excitement, and she nodded her head and said: "Yes, I do, Edwards, but you must first promise me never to tell tales to the other servants."

' "I promise I won't say a word to anyone," I gasped, and she gently squeezed my stiffie and replied: "Very well, then. Now let's see who can get undressed first!"

'We stripped off our clothes and I thought my cock was going to burst when Lady Maud exposed her exquisite bare breasts, each topped by a large rosy nipple. And when she lay down on the blanket, I could see the pouting pink lips of her cunney through her bushy thatch of silky pussey hair. I knelt down between Lady Maud's thighs and her roving fingers took possession of my prick, capping and uncapping my knob as she massaged my shaft with both hands.

'She murmured softly: "This is a huge cock for a boy of your age, quite large enough for a man in his prime. Such a smooth shaft, yet so hard and stiff to the touch. Have you ever used this noble tool for anything except tossing yourself off?"

' "Not since Noreen the scullerymaid left last month, ma'am," I panted breathlessly. "She used to rub it for me whilst I played with her titties, but this will be my first real fuck." Actually, this wasn't strictly true, for I had fucked Noreen, but I didn't want to give the girl a bad character, and furthermore, I correctly assumed that Lady Maud would get even more excited if she thought she would be plucking my cherry.

' "Ah, you sweet boy, I know I am going to enjoy this naughty adventure," she exclaimed, pulling me over her, and parting her legs. Then she opened up the entrance to her pouting red-lipped chink for me and inserted my knob between her yielding love lips. As it slipped into her welcoming love funnel, I sucked on her erect tawney nipples, moving my head from one to the other until we were both in a perfect frenzy of excitement.

' "More!" she cried out. "I want more!" and I fucked her as powerfully as I could, plunging my prick in and out of her wet pussey, my balls banging against her bottom as she raised her legs and wrapped them around my waist. My balls felt full to bursting but I managed to delay my ejaculation until Lady Maud squealed with delight, reaching her climax, and moments later I flooded her cunney with a torrent of sticky jism.

' "Well done, young Edwards, that was a divine spend," she said cheerfully as I lay slumped upon her soft curves. "But we had better get dressed, in case somebody comes along and sees us in a compromising position." '

Edwards smiled ruefully and concluded his racy confession by saying: 'I was walking on air for the next few days, because I guessed that Lady Maud would want me to fuck her again. But as things turned out, her husband returned home the following week and announced that he had been offered a high Government post in Ceylon, and I never had another opportunity to fuck her. When they sold up their home, I left her employ to come to London, and worked for two years for Lord Shuster before securing a position in this house with Colonel Wright.'

'Well, I know that you haven't lacked for female companionship since your arrival, and you will probably have the chance to enjoy some free time with Selina whilst I am away,' I said drily. 'All I ask is that you keep off the billards table!'

He gave a throaty laugh and said, 'We will, sir. I took your advice about having a quiet word with Mrs Riley and, as she put it, so long as I slip her a length now and then, she is quite happy to lend Selina and myself the use of her bed.'

'Splendid,' I said as he shut the lid of my trunk, and I went downstairs and to my shame polished off three toasted muffins for my tea.

In the morning, the alarm clock woke me from a deep, dreamless slumber, and I was ready to leave when, at half past eight precisely, the Prestoncrest driver knocked on the front door. Kitty Forrest was equally punctual and we arrived at Euston Station in good time to catch the express train to Liverpool. Naturally, the train was crowded with people going up North to see the Grand National, and even the first-class seats were at a premium. However, only two demure young ladies were sitting opposite us in our compartment when we pulled out of Euston, although I was able to gauge from the dockets on the two empty seats that these would be filled when the ticket-holders joined the train at Watford Junction.

'Would you care for a newspaper, Kitty?' I asked, as the locomotive wheezed its way up the steep gradient to the Primrose Hill tunnel. 'You may take your pick from *The Times*, *Daily News*, or the *Daily Mirror*.'

'No, thank you, Rupert. I am halfway through an exciting story in my magazine and I can hardly wait to finish it,' she replied. At the mention of my name, one of the girls seated opposite looked up and said, 'Excuse me, sir, I could not help overhearing your friend's reply. Would you be Mr Rupert Mountjoy of Bedford Square?'

'I am, indeed,' I replied with a slight bow of acknowledgement and, looking closer at the raven-haired young lady, I went on, 'You must forgive me, but although your face is familiar, I cannot quite remember where we met.'

'There is really nothing to forgive,' she replied, with a slight shrug of her shoulders. 'It is perhaps a mixed blessing, but since my childhood I have always enjoyed an extraordinarily good memory for people and places. We met fleetingly last September in the bar during the interval of *The Count of Luxembourg* at the Theatre Royal, Drury Lane. You were with your cousin Beresford, I recall, and my companion for the evening was my brother Radleigh, who was a contemporary of yours at Oxford.'

I pressed my fist against my forehead and exclaimed, 'Of course, you're Radleigh Thomson's sister and your name is – no, please don't tell me – I'll get it,' I said, screwing up my face as I concentrated all my energies in trying to remember the attractive girl's name. 'It's Valerie, is it not?' I added triumphantly, and was rewarded by a smile for my sterling mental efforts.

'How nice to meet you again, Miss Thomson. I trust you and Radleigh are keeping well. I must say that I haven't seen a great deal of him lately. May I introduce Miss Kitty Forrest to you?'

'A pleasure to meet you, Miss Forrest,' said Valerie Thomson as she shook hands with Kitty. 'And I would like you both to meet my dear friend, Miss Lettie Whorlsop. Lettie, as you heard, this gentleman is Mr Rupert Mountjoy.'

The extremely attractive blonde girl smiled and

extended her hand. 'How do you do, Mr Mount-joy? Do I take it that you and Miss Forrest are travelling up to Liverpool for the big race tomorrow afternoon?'

'Indeed, we are,' replied Kitty. 'Although Rupert and I are both staying at the Adelphi Hotel this evening, we have been invited by two different parties. He will be at the dinner given by the American racehorse owner, Mr Foxhall Keene, whilst I shall be a guest of Mr Gilbert Sharkey, the merchant banker.'

'Good heavens, he's also our host! And our two friends Jenny Temple and Yvonne Camberley-Hicks, who are joining the train at Watford, are also going to the same party,' exclaimed a startled Valerie Thomson. 'Knowing his reputation of being rather "fast", I wonder how many other girls Gilbert Sharkey has invited, and what entertainment he has in mind?'

'We shall soon find out,' said Kitty thoughtfully. 'I've only met the gentleman briefly, and was rather surprised to receive his invitation. But I understand that he does give rather splendid parties.'

I read my newspaper whilst the girls compared notes on Gilbert Sharkey, who was undoubtedly one of the most eligible young men in England. He was the second son of Sir Peter Sharkey QC, the famous barrister, but instead of following his father's footsteps into the law, the young Sharkey had taken an economics degree at Cambridge and, after gaining valuable experience with Rothschild's, climbed the ladder of success and became the managing director and joint owner of a highly profitable merchant bank in the City.

Then two years ago, at the relatively tender age of twenty-nine, Gilbert Sharkey announced his immediate retirement, and it soon became clear that he was going to spend his time in the pursuit of pleasure. Whilst his name was quickly linked with an ever-lengthening list of ladies, in the pages of *The Oyster*, a writer noted that Gilbert appeared to be trying to make up for the lost time when he had spent most of his waking hours on financial affairs. The scribe warned the dashing Mr Sharkey not to overstrain his supposedly extremely large penis!

As I pondered upon what Gilbert Sharkey had in mind for his Grand National shenanigans, the train pulled into Watford Junction and slowly shuddered to a halt. And, as Valerie Thomson had said, a few moments later the remaining seats in our compartment were taken by two more excited girls who had been invited to spend the weekend at the Adelphi Hotel at Gilbert Sharkey's expense. Valerie introduced the girls to Kitty and myself, and I rang for the attendant and ordered two bottles of chilled champagne to get us all in the mood for the forthcoming sporting weekend.

Despite my protestations, Lettie Whorlsop, the youngest daughter of the Whorlsop family which owned a well-known chain of grocery stores throughout Southern England, insisted on ordering two more bottles and by half past twelve we were all feeling rather merry, to say the least. We staggered into the restaurant car (which was fortunately only two carriages away) for the first luncheon call and drank more champagne with the meal. We had just passed Wolverhampton when, even more worse for wear, we returned back to our compartment.

'Right, now it's non-stop all the way to Liverpool, ladies,' I announced thickly, sliding into my seat. 'Kitty, I hope you and the other ladies will excuse me, but I'm going to take a little nap and I suggest that you all do the same.'

They chorused their agreement and in less than thirty seconds I was slumbering peacefully. Strangely enough, I dreamed that my prick was standing stiffly outside my trousers and that two soft hands were rubbing up and down the fully erect shaft. Then it felt as if a second pair of hands were busy unbuckling my belt and unbuttoning my fly. Next there was a rustle and I imagined that a body was forcing itself between my thighs and a small tongue swished wetly over the top of my helmet.

With a start I woke up, only to discover that the train had halted in a tunnel, and in the dim light of the compartment's sole working electric bulb I could see that Kitty was standing next to me holding my shaft in her hands, whilst the silky black hair on the head which was bobbing up and down on my cock belonged to Valerie Thomson. This was not the only sexual activity taking place, for on the seat opposite Lettie Whorlsop lay flat on her back, whilst on her knees between Lettie's parted legs was the slender boyish figure of Jenny

Temple who, her hands cupped around the wiggling cheeks of Lettie's bottom, was bending forward to suck greedily upon her engorged stiff nipples whilst her hand was jammed underneath the black cushion of hair between Lettie's thighs, and from the girl's convulsive jerks and her tiny sighs of joy, it was obvious that she was finger-fucking Lettie's pussey.

Combined with Kitty's slow yet insistent wanking of my shaft and the tip of Valerie's wicked tongue flicking around the ridges of my knob, this sensual sight swiftly brought me to a thundering climax, and the buxom figure of Yvonne (who must have been sitting in a corner watching this lustful scene) suddenly came forward and joined Valerie in licking up the flood of creamy seed which had spurted out of my cock.

With a piercing whistle we began to move slowly forward again, and I urged my lustful troupe of young ladies to dress themselves before we travelled out of the tunnel and into the daylight – and it was as well that they took my advice, for although we finally left the tunnel at some speed, a few miles later we were again stationary for some minutes alongside a south-bound train whose occupants could clearly see us through our uncurtained window.

We lurched forward, passed some workers who were repairing a stretch of track, and again picked up speed. But as we rattled over a set of points and roared through Crewe, I saw Lettie bring a prick-sized ladies' comforter out of her handbag and, raising her skirt, the brazen hussey remarked that it was well she had not put her knickers back on because Jenny had not had the time to finish her off when the train had begun to move again after the fortuitous stop in the tunnel.

'Don't fuss, Rupert,' said Valerie, who was also enjoying the sight of the dildo sliding in and out of Lettie's pretty pussey. 'She needs to spend, and as you said, it's non-stop now all the way.'

'Let me help you, dear, I see you're using the instrument modelled on the prick of your fellow West Country friend, the writer Jeffrey Long-fellow,' said Jenny, leaning down to take hold of the white china cock, and, looking up, she winked at me and added, 'Lettie comes from Somerset, and we often call her "The Wookey Hole" when she gets too randy.'

'Don't be such a tease,' panted Lettie. 'Why don't you use your lips for a more useful purpose than making silly jokes?'

'Oh, all right,' said Jenny good-humouredly. 'Gather round everyone, just in case we do stop again before Liverpool.'

I stood directly in front of her and the other girls formed a circle around Jenny as she knelt between Lettie's legs and threw up the girl's skirt to expose her delectable pussey to my lascivious gaze. Lettie closed her eyes and stretched out her legs as Jenny began to stimulate her cunney, pulling open her love lips and rubbing her knuckles back and forth across the moistening crack until the girl's body quivered with unslaked desire. Then she eased a finger into her cunt, and

Lettie sighed and raised up her bottom. This finger was joined by another, and then a third as Jenny slid her head forward, and still working her fingers, squishing in and out of Lettie's juicy honeypot, she kissed her puffy cunney lips and slid her pink tongue between them.

'Oooh, that's divine,' gurgled Lettie when the tip of Jenny's fluttering tongue found the edge of her swelling clitty. 'Suck harder, darling, suck harder and make me spend!'

Jenny responded at once, clutching Lettie's thighs as she thrust her face deeper against her hairy cunt, and I could hear her suck and slurp with great vigour, and smell the pungent cuntal juice which was now flowing freely from Lettie's sopping quim. I moved forward to watch this voluptuous tribadic display at even closer quarters and saw Jenny pass her tongue lasciviously up and down the slightly parted crimson lips, and then I could also see Lettie's stiff fleshy clitty which now projected a good two inches out from her cunt.

'Yes, yes,yes!' shrieked Lettie as Jenny took her love button between her lips and playfully rolled it around her mouth. Then, after receiving one last sweep round from Jenny's tongue, Lettie started to spend. Her hips bucked violently and then from her pussey spurted a fine creamy emission which splattered over Jenny's face and flooded her mouth as she ground her slit against Jenny's open mouth until the blissful ecstasy began to fade and her body shuddered into limpness, heaving and panting with exhaustion as the delicious crisis ebbed slowly away.

As was to be expected, when I straightened up and went back to my seat, my shaft was forming a tent in the front of my trousers, but we were only twenty minutes from Lime Street Station, and Amber Berlynne would be waiting for me either there or at the hotel. So whilst I was greatly tempted to present my prick to any one of the girls who might oblige with either a quick knee-trembler or another gobble, I recalled Dr Letchmore's words on the perils of over-indulgence and took out *The Expenses Account*, a skilfully crafted novel by one Mr Terence Jackson, which I had purchased at the bookstall on Euston Station.

I had just finished the first chapter when we arrived in Liverpool. There was a bevy of porters on the platform and one beefy 'Scouser' pushed forward to assist Kitty as she alighted, so I gave him the job of placing all of our luggage on one of the three motor charabancs which the Adelphi Hotel had hired to meet the train.

'Thank you very much, sir,' said the porter when I gave him a florin [2s. – *Editor*]. 'May fortune smile on your horse in the big race.'

'You wouldn't happen to have heard anything of interest about tomorrow?' I asked, as he gave Kitty a helping hand into the charabanc. 'I know you chaps keep your ears to the ground.'

'I've heard there's big money going on Johnstown Lad, but the National's such a lottery,' he replied with a shrug. 'The London punters fancy the King's horse, Flaxman, but I don't rate it myself. What do you fancy, sir?'

'You could do worse than put a small each-way stake on Rubio, but don't bet any more than a Saturday night's drinking money,' I said.

The porter looked at me with a horrified expression. 'Oh, I wouldn't bet as much as that, but the rent man might have to wait a week or longer than usual if the worst comes to the worse.'

I chuckled and boarded the bus for the short journey across the square to the hotel where, as I guessed, Amber Berlynne was waiting for me in the reception area. She was standing by the arrivals desk, brushing a stray strand of her beautiful blonde hair from her face, and when I pointed her out to my travelling companion, Kitty Forrest commented, 'What a ravishing young girl, Rupert! No wonder you journeyed two hundred miles to see her. I congratulate you on your taste.'

Amber's bright blue eyes lit up when she saw me, and she ran towards us and then unselfconsciously rushed straight into my arms.

'Hello, darling, long time, no see,' I said easily, kissing her cheek. 'Let me have a good look at you, Amber – it's been far too long since I've seen you in the flesh.'

'Yes, and except for my occasional hurried visits to London, you've seen very little of me in the flesh since that wonderful holiday in Devon last summer,' murmured the delicious girl as she slid her hand under my jacket and across my chest. 'So we must seize this opportunity and make up for all that lost time.' [*For an explicit account of Rupert's liaison with Amber Berlynne, see*

I kissed her sweet little nose and said, 'Quite, so, but first I must register and have my luggage taken up to my room. Oh, and let me introduce you to Miss Kitty Forrest, who travelled up with me from London. She is also staying at the Adelphi, but as a guest of the famous Gilbert Sharkey, who apparently is throwing a big party here this evening.'

Amber looked closely at Kitty as the two girls shook hands, and then she said, 'Miss Forrest, your face is very familiar. Where have I seen you before? Oh, yes, I know! Wasn't your photograph on the front cover of *Harmsworth's Magazine* last month?'

Kitty nodded her head. 'Yes, and you can also see me in the current edition of *The Bystander*,' she replied as we walked towards the reception desk. 'You see, I need to augment my annual allowance from my father, who is only a modestly paid rural dean down in Herefordshire, so I work as a model for Society photographers who use my portrait for their windows, and sell their prints to picture editors of the weekly journals. 'I am also employed very occasionally by a commercial agency – in next week's *Everybody's* I appear in an advertisement for Kishawe and Raoul's Bois de Santal Toilet Soap, whilst next month you will see a photograph of me mixing the ingredients for a pudding in a new cookery book written by the famous culinary expert, Mrs Hetty Beaconsfield.'

'Heavens, I had no idea that you were so

famous,' I said, and she chuckled and said, 'Infamous, more like! Although, after my picture appeared in *John Bull* last October, I received almost fifty letters from gentlemen requesting an autographed photograph, preferably the one of me in the French bathing costume which appeared in the magazine!'

'I'm not surprised,' said Amber, who was confident enough of her own good looks not to be jealous of another attractive girl. 'But I'm truly sorry that you are not with our party, Miss Forrest, because there is a well-known artist amongst our guests who I am certain would be greatly interested in having you sit for him. He needs a beautiful new face such as yours to show in an important exhibition of his work at a famous London gallery later this year. May I tell him of your arrival?'

'Of course you may, and thank you for the kind compliment,' smiled Kitty, signing the visitors' register. 'If this gentleman wishes to contact me, I am in room 119. Now I am sure that our paths will cross some time tonight, but for the present I will leave you and Rupert to your own devices, for I gather you have plenty to occupy yourselves with till this evening!'

She shook hands with us and made her way up to her room, whilst I registered and the clerk gave me the key to room 421. Amber accompanied me up in the elevator and stayed with me whilst we waited for my luggage to be brought up.

After the porter had left, depositing my bags on the stand, Amber kissed me on the lips, kicked off her shoes, then slipped off her jacket and said brightly, 'Darling, shall I help you unpack?'

'By all means,' I rejoined as Amber began to unbutton her blouse. 'But if you take off any more clothes I don't think it will be worthwhile even looking for the keys of my trunk.'

'No, I wouldn't bother,' agreed Amber, unhooking her skirt and letting it fall to the floor. 'The sensible thing to do would be to take off your suit and hang it up in the wardrobe so it doesn't get creased. Meanwhile, I'll fold my clothes over this chair.'

I could not prevent a low growl of excitement escaping from my throat when Amber pulled her chemise over her head and I gazed at the firm swell of her bare breasts. The globes proudly uptilted and crowned with pink circled aureoles and raised raspberry nipples acted like magnets to my gleaming eyes.

'As I said downstairs, we have a great deal of wasted time to make up,' Amber said huskily as, clad only in a pair of open-legged drawers of semi-transparent *crêpe de Chine*, through which I could make out the outline of her pubic bush, she walked purposefully towards me and offered up her mouth to be kissed whilst deftly unbuckling my belt and unhooking the catch on the front of my trousers.

Our lips crushed together and we melted into a burning kiss, our tongues filling the other's mouth, probing, rousing and caressing. I wrapped my arms around the exquisite fair-haired nymph and within seconds we had divested ourselves of all our remaining clothes and our naked bodies writhed from side to side as we tossed and turned in each other's arms on the soft bed. My hands moved to cup Amber's beautiful breasts whilst she grasped my hot rock-hard prick and gently squeezed the throbbing shaft. Then her lips broke away to travel downwards towards my aching tool and when she kissed all around it, my cock shook with frustration. I whimpered in disappointment as Amber teased her tongue along the insides of my thighs. However, I had only a short time to wait for with a sensuous giggle she took pity on me and as I looked down upon the tousled mass of flaxen hair between my legs, her tongue shot out and swirled around the underside of my rampant rod.

'A-r-g-h! My God, that's marvellous,' I groaned in sheer ecstasy as, after a swift lick on my purple helmet, Amber opened her mouth and proceeded to suck at least four inches of my twitching tool in between her ruby red lips. I was in the very seventh heaven of delight as her moist mouth worked up and down on my sated shaft, licking and lapping every inch of my entire length, her hand gripping the base as, keeping her lips taut, she pumped her head to and fro, sucking lustily and pausing only to lap up some pre-cum juice which had oozed out of my knob.

Now one of her hands started to gently massage my tightening ballsack as she jammed her mouth over the mushroom dome of my bell-end and slurped away with even greater intensity. The sensation was just too overpowering and I knew that it was simply impossible to delay the inexorable rush of sperm shooting up from my balls. So with a hoarse cry I jerked my hips upwards and sent a spray of creamy seed spurting into Amber's mouth. She swallowed the first spunky squirt and with a delighted gurgle, the lovely girl gulped down the remainder of my copious emission until my shaft finally ceased its frenzied agitation.

I expelled a deep breath as I sank down on to the pillow but my tool remained erect in her mouth as she washed over my knob with her tongue. Then Amber released my glistening cock from between her lips, but kept hold of my still stiff shaft and she fell back to lie beside me.

'Make love to me, Rupert. I can hardly wait to feel your wonderful thick cock inside my wet little cunney,' she whispered, arching her body like a sleek kitten as I scrambled to my knees and positioned myself between her superbly sculpted thighs.

I began by kissing Amber's toes, feet and ankles before progressing upwards to her knees whilst my hands slid upwards to massage her divinely rounded breasts. She parted her legs to expose her silky flaxen bush and pink cunney lips, between which her excited little clitty was already jutting out like a miniature cock. And she purred with pleasure when I buried my head between her thighs and sucked deeply on her juicy, open cunt.

'Y-e-s-s! Y-e-s-s! Y-e-s-s!' she panted as I flicked my tongue in and out between her rolled love lips, nipping the fleshy bud of her clitty with my teeth as I tweaked her rubbery nipples between my fingers before sliding my arms around her body and downwards to grasp her jiggling buttocks.

Amber gave a tiny scream as, inhaling the tangy feminine aroma from her pussey, I slipped my tongue inside her dripping crack, licking rhythmically away in long, sweeping strokes. Her love juices flowed over my tongue and she moaned, 'Oh, fuck me, Rupert, I want you to fuck me with that big thick todger, you naughty boy!'

She shuddered as I flicked her clitty one more time before pulling myself up, turning the trembling girl face downwards upon the eiderdown. Then I reached out and placed a pillow under her belly, so that her enchanting bum cheeks were raised high in the air. Then, gripping my quivering cock in my hand, I nudged her legs apart and looked down on both the wrinkled starfish-shaped rosette of her rear dimple and the pouting love lips of her pussey which were both waiting to herald the arrival of my pulsating prick.

Fortunately, I did not have to make the difficult choice of which path to follow, because Amber turned her pretty face round to give me a large wink, and then said with a saucy grin, 'Oooh, I'm looking forward to this – I'm glad you remembered that I adore being fucked doggie-style. But please don't go up my bum, Rupert, I want to feel every inch of your lovely tool in my tight little notch. You don't mind too much, do you?'

'I don't mind in the slightest,' I gasped, sliding my knob into the cleft between her jiggling bum cheeks. 'My preference has always been for pussey, though I'll happily go through the tradesmen's entrance now and then, because variety is the spice of life.'

'Off you go, then,' she giggled as, with great care, I slowly guided my knob into her sopping slit from behind, easing my shaft into her welcoming wetness until her bum cheeks were nestling against my thighs. Then I leaned forward so that my hairy chest was pressed against her back, and reached round and fondled her delectable bosoms, clutching each in a firm grip as I started to slick my prick in and out of her juicy cunt.

This fired Amber to move her hips in a fierce sensual rhythm so that, with every plunge forward, my shaft was fully ensheathed in her warm, clinging wetness. Her wiggling backside spurred me on to even faster and deeper thrusts and as my shaft slid to and fro along the lubricated walls of her love channel, I could feel my foreskin being drawn backwards and forwards with every shove. Now I might have been well serviced in recent days by a bevy of willing girls, but this was a magnificent, truly memorable fuck of the highest quality! What delicious ripples seeped through every fibre of my being whilst I pumped my trustly tool in and out of her squelchy quim! By this time, the seed was already boiling up in my balls, so I was more than ready when Amber shrieked out, 'Now! Now! Shoot your spunk into my cunney!'

With a long loud groan I pistoned my prick in up to the hilt inside Amber's cunt and discharged a powerful jet of frothy jism inside her willing slit. At the same time she started to clutch wildly at the sheets and moan loudly into her pillow, shivering all over as the exquisite force of her own orgasm swept through her. As she spent, I managed one last thrust forward and my balls slapped against Amber's bum cheeks as I shot a final spasm of sticky spunk into her flooded cunt before collapsing on top of the sweet girl, both our bodies now bathed in perspiration.

We lay still for a while, and then Amber sat up and planted a light kiss on my now shrunken shaft. 'Goodness gracious, Rupert, I'm glad to see that your cock hasn't forgotten how to perform, though no doubt it has not been short of a nice moist pussey whilst you have been gallivanting around the West End. Now I suggest we have a bath and wash away the stains of that glorious fuck. I'll go into the bathroom and turn on the taps.'

'That's a good idea, sweetheart, and if you're a good girl I'll soap your back,' I called out as I heard the rumble of water cascading into the bath, which was of so large a design that Amber and I could lie comfortably together in the warm water.

'Who is this artist with our party?' I asked idly as I splashed some water over her shoulders. 'Don't tell me it's the infamous Eric Marks.'

'Well, yes. But you mustn't feel jealous simply

because I allowed him to spout his seed over my tits,' replied Amber coyly. 'Just remember that if I were to take umbrage over every girl you have poked, I would hardly be able to carry on a conversation with any female under thirty in London Society!'

'*Touché*! I withdraw the adjective "infamous" and substitute "randy",' I chuckled. 'I know he would fuck Kitty Forrest at the drop of a sketchpad, but do you really believe he might want to paint her portrait?'

'Certainly I do, and I think Eric would pay her handsomely, for not only has she the most lovely features, but her face is already known to many people and he would know that there would be many fast young men about town who would want to buy her picture, should he decide to put it up for sale.'

I considered this remark and realised that there was probably much in her argument. 'In that case, do introduce Kitty to Mr Marks – she probably needs the money,' I said, climbing out of the bath and wrapping myself in a bath towel. 'And whilst you are at it, introduce me as well. I'd like to meet this chap who appears to poke all the girls he portrays on canvas.'

'With pleasure, although won't you feel irritated if Kitty is attracted to him?' asked Amber mischievously as I held open a bath towel for her.

'Now who is being distrustful?' I said lightly smacking her bottom. 'Kitty and I are mere acquaintances.' And I went on to explain how we had happened to meet when I fished her friend

Claudia's shoe out of the pond in Regent's Park.

Although Amber was not over-possessive, this answer nevertheless pleased her, and she said she would speak to Eric Marks before dinner and arrange for Kitty and he to meet somewhere more private than one of the hotel's luxuriously furnished public rooms. 'I'll ask them both up to my suite at six-thirty, Rupert. You'll also want to be there, won't you? Its room number 312.'

When she had dried herself, Amber put on her clothes and called, first Kitty, and then Eric on the internal telephone. They were both pleased to go along with her plan and in turn, she was equally happy to agree to Eric's request to change the venue for our pre-dinner drinks to his room, where he had already set up an easel.

After Amber left to go back to her room, I began to unpack my case myself, for I could not be bothered to ring for one of the hotel's valets. Whilst I was unlocking my trunk, I noticed that there was an envelope addressed to me on the dressing table. I opened the envelope and found that it contained a warm typewritten note of welcome signed by my host, Mr Foxhall Keene, informing me that as many of the guests were travelling long distances this afternoon, he would suggest we use the afternoon to recover from our journeys and, if we so desired, to take tea in our rooms. In the meantime, he looked forward to greeting us in person at a reception in the Sir Reginald Green suite, beginning at seven forty-five, with dinner to be served at eight-thirty. This was most considerate of Mr Keene, and after I had finished unpacking, I decided to forgo tea. Instead, I slipped on a fresh set of underwear and settled down on the bed for a rest, since all the fucking and sucking on the train with the girls and the sensational coupling with Amber had quite tired me out. I was already struggling to keep my eyes open when my head hit the pillow.

However, after a nice nap, I started to leaf through the volume of artistic poses by the German photographer Oskar Treuhertz, which my chum Frank Folkestone had recently sent me from Paris. Edwards had not told me that he had packed this book and I was very glad that I had not ordered the services of a valet, for the pictures were amongst the most erotic I had ever seen. All the women shown were extremely attractive and most of them were caught by Herr Treuhertz in the most lascivious situations that one could imagine.

There was one particular photograph which took my fancy – a beautiful half-caste girl was shown lying across the belly of an equally nude dark-skinned gentleman sitting in a reclining chair. He was in the act of administering a friendly slap on her chubby bum cheeks with one hand, whilst in front of them another dusky unclothed beauty knelt at his side, her hands holding his huge erect prick and her face pressed against this colossal cock and her tongue sliding across his uncapped knob.

'I wouldn't mind taking his place for an hour or two,' I murmured softly to myself, and then I almost jumped out of my skin when a sweet feminine voice broke into my reverie and chimed out, 'And I wouldn't mind taking one of those girl's places either!'

I jumped off the bed in a state of shock, but fortunately I had not been disturbed by one of these sneak thieves who specialise into breaking into hotel bedrooms, but only by a cheery young chambermaid who, trying hard to suppress her giggles, apologised profusely for startling me. 'I'm here to turn down the bed, sir. I did knock on the door, but you must have been so engrossed in your book that you didn't hear me.'

'That's all right, no damage done,' I said as I watched the coltish young girl perform her duties. 'And if you want to look more closely at this book, you're welcome to come back tomorrow evening.'

'I might take you up on that offer, Mr Mountjoy,' she said, and she winked at me as she flounced out of the room. Good show, I thought, as I swiftly finished dressing. A nice little kiss and cuddle with this friendly girl would make up for the financial losses I fully expected to make the next day at the racecourse, especially as from past experience I knew that Amber was far from averse to taking part in a voluptuous 'three-in-a-bed' affair.

So I was feeling well contented when I met Kitty Forrest in the elevator. She looked ravishing in a pink satin gown, and I said to her, 'Good evening, Kitty. Let me escort you to Eric Marks's suite.' As we walked down the corridor, I added, 'You look absolutely exquisite, if I may say so.'

'Thank you, kind sir. I hope that Mr Marks will

think so too,' she replied. Then I knocked on the door, which was opened by Amber, who also looked stunning in a daringly low-cut azure blue silk dress.

'Hello there, you two. Do come in. Eric won't be a moment, he is just taking off his trousers to sign the sketch he made this morning of Mr Foxhall Keene's daughter,' she said mysteriously, and we followed her into the artist's suite.

'Why would he have to undress to sign a picture?' I enquired, but it was Kitty who answered my question. With a slight note of reproach in her voice, she said, 'Rupert, I'm surprised you didn't know that Eric Marks is a member of this new social impressionist school of painting. I'll let Mr Marks explain the ideas of the movement himself, but one of their trademarks which signifies their rejection of traditional artistic values is to sign their works not with an ordinary brush, but by the use of a finger, a toe, or some other part of the anatomy to daub their initials on the left-hand corner of the pictures.'

'Cocking a snook at the Establishment, so to speak,' I said.

'Exactly so,' Amber replied with a gay laugh. 'And you really could not have chosen a more appropriate phrase as far as Eric is concerned. He is one of the radicals who signs his name by dipping his erect shaft into a pot of paint and using his prick as a paintbrush.'

'You're pulling my leg,' I said roundly, but the giggling girl insisted that she was telling the truth, the whole truth and nothing but the truth.

215

Nevertheless, I continued to find it difficult to believe her. 'Very well then,' I said, 'I'll confront Mr Marks when he comes in from the bedroom, and we'll see if he confirms what you say.' Frankly, I thought this would make them confess that they were playing a joke on me, but instead, with a fresh burst of laughter when she saw me struggle as I weighed up whether or not I was being taken for a ride, Amber said, 'Why wait till then, Rupert? If you still doubt my word, I'm sure that Eric won't mind if you go in and watch him in action.'

'All right, I will,' I said, and I walked across to the door and called out, 'Mr Marks, it's Rupert Mountjoy here. May I please speak with you for a moment about an artistic principle?'

'Of course you may. Come on in,' he shouted back and so, with both Amber and Kitty at my shoulder, I flung open the door . . .

TO BE CONTINUED . . .

This story will be continued in The Intimate Memoirs of An Edwardian Dandy VI: A Game Little Filly, which will be published in May 1995. However, Rupert Mountjoy's many fans might like to know that Rubio, the horse he was told to back by his family's old manservant, did indeed win the 1908 Grand National at 66 to 1!